2040 A.D.

■

Oakland, California,
United States
Page 67

Seltjarnarnes, Iceland
Page 131

New York City, New York
United States
Page 8

San Francisco, California,
United States
Page 6

Ohio, United States
Page 147

Mexico City, Mexico
Page 49

Zagreb, Croatia
Page 111

Uttarakhand, India
Page 99

Singapore
Page 15

Istanbul, Turkey
Page 89

Somewhere in the
Northern Hemisphere
Page 77

Far North Queensland,
Australia
Page 35

This book was printed using chlorine-free, 100 percent post-consumer waste paper. Using this paper has saved 39 fully grown trees, 3,100 gallons of water, 16 million BTUs of energy, 130 pounds of solid waste, and 16,700 pounds of greenhouse gases.

© 2019 McSweeney's Quarterly Concern and the contributors, San Francisco, California. ASSISTED BY: Ellie Bozmarova, Madison Decter, Annie Dills, Colin Heasley, Kitania Folk, Miranda LeGate, Casey Leidig, Emma Theiss. WEB DEVELOPMENT: Brian Christian. SALES AND DISTRIBUTION MANAGER: Dan Weiss. PUBLISHING ASSOCIATE: Eric Cromie. ART DIRECTOR: Sunra Thompson. COPY EDITOR: Daniel Levin Becker. FOUNDING EDITOR: Dave Eggers. EXECUTIVE DIRECTOR: Amanda Uhle. EDITOR: Claire Boyle.

Scientific advisors: Natural Resources Defense Council (NRDC), with special thanks to Elizabeth Corr, Rob Moore, Dr. Kim Knowlton, Anna Weber, Lisa Speer, Kate Poole, Juanita Constible, Arohi Sharma, and Susan Casey-Lefkowitz.

Additional NRDC assistance: Nora Mango, Fabi Nunez, Jeff Turrentine, Michelle Bright, Caroline Craig, Chris Tacket, Ben Smith, Kim Morasse, Tejal Mankad, Daniel Hinerfeld, Cheryl Slean.

COVER AND INTERIOR ILLUSTRATIONS: Wesley Allsbrook.

Printed in Canada.

Introduction *by Susan Casey-Lefkowitz,* *Chief Program Officer, Natural Resources Defense Council*	New York City, New York, United States	8
The Rememberers *by Rachel Heng*	Singapore	15
Drones Above the Coral Sand *by Claire G. Coleman*	Far North Queensland, Australia	35
The Night Drinker *by Luis Alberto Urrea*	Mexico City, Mexico	49
New Jesus *by Tommy Orange*	Oakland, California United States	67
The Good Plan *by Mikael Awake*	Somewhere in the Northern Hemisphere	77
He Are the People *by Elif Shafak*	Istanbul, Turkey	89
Ghost Town *by Kanishk Tharoor*	Uttarakhand, India	99
1740 *by Asja Bakić*	Zagreb, Croatia	111
To Everything, Tern Tern Tern *by Birna Anna Björnsdóttir*	Seltjarnarnes, Iceland	131
Save Yourself *by Abbey Mei Otis*	Ohio, United States	147

37°45'34.5"N

TWENTY YEARS AGO, *THE SOPRANOS* won its first Golden Globe. Mad cow disease was ripping through Europe. George W. Bush had just been elected president. If those events feel as recent to you as they do to us, you'll see our point: twenty years wasn't that long ago. So it would follow that, similarly, twenty years isn't that far into the future either. That's why we were rattled when we read the climate report the United Nations released in 2018. The study warned that the planet will reach a point of no return if we allow the global temperature to rise more than another half-degree Celsius. And if it continues at its current rate, the report added, that could happen by the year 2040. Twenty years. *You thought it was bad now?* the report seemed to ask. *Just wait till 2040.*

These chilling forecasts were hard to wrap our minds around, so we enlisted some of the best writers we know and asked them to envision what 2040 might look like in the event that we don't right the ship.

As jumping-off points for their stories, we assigned each author a specific climate event that appears in the report–coral reef destruction, swells of climate refugees, and dangerous heat waves, to name a few. Digging through pages and pages of scientific reports, though, we realized we were in over our heads. So we brought on the brilliant people at the Natural Resources Defense Council (NRDC) as collaborators, and that's when the project really took shape.

NRDC connected each author with a consulting expert hand-chosen to provide a scientific backbone for their story. At the same time, we felt strongly about giving the writers free rein to determine how closely they adhered to that science–or even, for that matter, to realism at all. This collection is, first and foremost, fiction. There's intergalactic travel, time travel, extreme life-extension, cults subsuming full civilizations. While it may not be a perfect scientific record, the great thing about this ever-expanding genre, climate fiction, is that it's free to reach into the weird and unverified places that science can't, to get at the urgency of the moment not through measurements but through something more intuitive. Over and over, these stories ask: if this worst-case projection for 2040 comes true, how will it disturb our closest relationships? Our capacity for sacrifice? Our connection to faith?

Though the authors were all assigned distinct topics, they unknowingly wrote toward a common center. Droughts welcome forest fires; melting ice caps bring coastal flooding brings climate migration brings food shortages. Because ultimately, the planet's ecosystems are profoundly interlocked–and we as citizens of it are, in turn, similarly fastened to each other.

Too often, the networks underlying a system become visible only when they malfunction. If we wait until 2040 to understand our planet's crucial equilibrium, it'll be too late. So we have a small window. It's closing very, very quickly, and much of the damage already done is permanent. But if we act immediately and push for sweeping change, we can hope that when today's children grow up, this collection will be a relic from a moment in which we almost took the wrong road, but didn't. ■ —CLAIRE BOYLE, EDITOR, McSWEENEY'S QUARTERLY

by Susan Casey-Lefkowitz
Chief Program Officer
Natural Resources Defense Council

40°44'26.4"N

TO WORK IN THE CLIMATE movement, as I've been doing for three decades now, is to learn how to move between poles of anxiety and hope without losing balance or focus. Nearly every week brings with it news of how communities around the globe are being adversely affected by the impacts of climate change. In just the past two years, the United States and the Caribbean have been hit by six record-setting hurricanes; the state of California has experienced some of the most intense wildfires in its history; a pair of cyclones, spaced just weeks apart, has devastated the African island of Mozambique; and Europe has been gripped by heat waves that have broken temperature records all across the continent. These events—and many others not listed here, but no less calamitous—are all geophysical symptoms of our inability to reduce carbon emissions.

But every week also brings with it the renewed need to inspire and mobilize people: to make sure they understand that while the hour is late, it's not *too* late. Though climate change is an indisputable aspect of the present day, we still have time to lessen its future impacts by dramatically lowering our emissions, and by simultaneously working to make sure that our communities and surrounding ecosystems are becoming more resilient to these impacts. To paraphrase the environmental scientist John Holdren, who served as President Obama's senior science advisor, we must learn how to "avoid the unmanageable and manage the unavoidable."

By allowing the planet to warm one degree Celsius above preindustrial levels, we've already ushered in an era of extreme and unprecedented weather events. To acknowledge this as a basic fact is sobering enough. But events over the last several years have made it even harder for some to remain hopeful. Before November of 2016, for example, few people would have expected the President of the United States to go out of his way to publicly sabotage an internationally celebrated climate treaty. Yet that's exactly what happened the following year, when President Donald Trump arrogantly and recklessly pulled our country out of the Paris Agreement, making many of us feel like we had gone through the looking glass. In an instant, the U.S. government went from leading the global climate effort to showing an utter contempt for it.

Against this backdrop, new studies are regularly being published to remind us of the price we've already paid, and how that price could well continue to rise. In May of 2019, the United Nations released a forty-page summary of its upcoming *Global Assessment Report on Biodiversity and Ecosystem Services*, detailing how human activity over the past few centuries has placed more than a million plant and animal species at risk of extinction. Its authors made clear that people–through the choices we've made relating to agriculture, deforestation, and the production and consumption of fossil fuels–have managed to generate the gravest threat to biodiversity in human history.

Another breathtaking document, released seven months earlier, left many activists, advocates, and ordinary climate-conscious individuals feeling temporarily paralyzed. In its *Special Report on Global Warming of 1.5°C*, the United Nations-sponsored Intergovernmental Panel on Climate Change (IPCC) painted a grim picture of our planet's future should human beings allow the planet to warm by another half-degree Celsius. If we can't keep that from happening by 2030, the report's authors warned, what we now think of as the worst effects of climate change will effectively be "baked in" to our natural systems by 2040–with no way for us to turn things around. And in a world where natural disasters have become everyday occurrences, they note, we can expect to see a commensurate rise in social and political disasters like famine, epidemics, mass migration, and regional conflict.

In our darkest moments–when we're reminded of how much damage we've already done to our planet, and how much more damage we might still do if we don't get a handle on our carbon emissions–the impulse to give up hope is an understandable one. But in the wake of so many setbacks and so much bad news, my climate-movement colleagues and I have witnessed something truly remarkable. Once the shock has worn off and people have had a chance to absorb the prognosis, they haven't given up. Instead, amazingly, they've *stepped* up.

In Europe last year, a fifteen-year-old activist named Greta Thunberg began camping out in front of the Swedish parliament building every day, demanding stronger climate policies from lawmakers and refusing to go to school until she got them; her singular act of protest quickly blossomed into an international youth movement, millions strong, dedicated to making sure that governments put climate action at the top of their priorities lists. Last February, after Thunberg gave a stirring speech to members of a major European Union advisory group in Brussels, Jean-Claude Juncker, the head of the E.U., took to the podium and announced that fully one-quarter of the E.U.'s budget would soon be going toward mitigating climate change. In his own speech, Juncker cited as a catalyzing force the movement that Thunberg started.

All over the world, in fact, elected officials and ordinary citizens alike have responded to the incontrovertible evidence of climate change by declaring their readiness to meet the epochal challenge it poses. Governments are investigating new and improved ways to rapidly decrease, and ultimately to eliminate, their carbon outputs. Communities are learning how better to adapt to the fact of rising sea levels, and how to ensure the safety of their most vulnerable members from heat waves, droughts, storms, and wildfires. Doing all of these things, nearly everyone acknowledges, will require massive investments in technology and infrastructure, a new focusing of political will, the restructuring of economies, and the reconfiguring of global alliances.

To this list I'd add one more requirement: imagination. In order to understand the totality of climate change—its causes, its effects, and its potential antidotes—we have to be able to visualize its ominous progress over time. Scientists consistently confirm what we can plainly see with our own eyes: that climate change is happening all around us, right now, in the form of altered weather patterns, rising seas, and skyrocketing summer temperatures. Their computerized models suggest how it might evolve in the near future, under certain conditions, and those models are crucial to our understanding of the issue. Still, human beings are storytelling animals. Data can persuade us, but it takes stories to move us.

And right now we need more people—millions more—to feel moved enough to take action. That's why my organization, the Natural Resources Defense Council (NRDC), didn't hesitate to say yes when we were asked if we wanted to work with the editors of *Timothy McSweeney's Quarterly Concern* on a special issue wholly devoted to climate change. NRDC has long been committed to reducing emissions and addressing the root causes of global warming; more recently, we've been working to help communities adapt to sea-level rise, flooding, extreme heat, and other manifestations of climate change that have a negative impact on public health. In the stories you're about to read, writers from around the world have taken turns imagining what our planet could look like in the year 2040: the same year that scientists believe humanity could reach the point of no return.

I'm typing these words in July of 2019. A girl born today will turn twenty-one in the summer of 2040. The stories in this issue combine to depict one version of reality—not the only one, but a plausible one—that potentially awaits her on the cusp of adulthood. Arctic communities are reeling from the ecosystemic stress of ice melt and drastic weather shifts. In India, unbearably oppressive heat waves have melted together until they're no longer discrete weather events but simply the way things are: deadly and routine. Other points around the globe have come to be defined by the way climate change has transformed them: a water-stressed American Midwest; a perpetually flooded Singapore; a Mexico unequipped to handle a massive influx of climate refugees.

Each story in this special issue is the product of a unique collaboration between its author and an NRDC policy expert with specialized knowledge of how climate change is already affecting the world, and how it could continue to affect the world in the decades to come. The result, we hope, is a collection where fiction's already considerable power is fortified by science. At the moment it still feels like an experiment; but these types of collaborations, I believe, will only become more common as artists and storytellers recognize a goal that they share with climate advocates: moving people to think and act differently. We all need to see what our future may or may not look like, depending on what choices we make as a global community. Writers and other artists—those of us who imagine things for a living, or as a calling—will prove to be indispensable partners in this effort.

That future doesn't have to be dystopian, even if much of contemporary climate fiction relies on dystopian imagery for its emotional impact. We also need to see writers and artists marshaling all of their narrative and descriptive skills to imagine a future where human beings come together, as a single species, to mitigate climate change's onslaught and reverse its course. Because let's face it: that future is the only one that any of us would ever want to live in.

It's ours, if we want it badly enough. I know that I want it; it's what keeps me from letting despair win out over hope. I know that our young people want it; it's what compels them to take to the streets by the millions, demanding climate action and climate justice for their generation and all generations to come.

Our climate story thus far has been frightening and inspiring, infuriating and empowering. It's been suspenseful in some ways and all too predictable in others. But we get to craft our own ending. And that ending, fortunately, has yet to be written. ■

THE
REMEMBERERS
by Rachel Heng

"RUBBER SEEDS," MA SAYS. "WHEN we visit my cousins, in the swa teng–"

"Countryside," the woman with the tablet says. "Please try to use standard English. The best results are achieved that way."

"Swa teng, countryside, aiya you know lah. I ask you before, you are Hokkien, right, girl?"

From the way a certain tendon in the woman's neck twitches I can tell she does not like being called girl, nor being reminded again of the question that Ma asks her at the start of every single session. The woman's name is Ms. Tan, a nothing of a name, but I would know her skinny moon face anywhere, I've spent so many Remembering sessions staring at it.

"Rubber seeds," I say. I touch Ma's shoulder, and the light pressure is enough to bring her back.

"We always collect them. My cousins' house there, a lot of rubber trees, you can find the seeds lying around just like that on the floor, so many! Ah, when we find one, we take it and rub against the wall–"

MCS58

"Wall?" Ms. Tan inquires.

"Any wall also can, just needs to be brick or concrete. The front of the house, the well, last time they get water from the well you know, so poor thing, Ah Bee every morning must wake up and go and take the water, so heavy, her arms become so thick, so muscular, like boy like that."

I see Ms. Tan's chest rise ever so slightly then fall, a wisp of a sigh that she keeps inside her. The session is not going well. In Ma's early sessions she was eager to please, flushed and bright-eyed at the novelty of having an audience, worried, perhaps, that they would stop listening if she said the wrong thing. It seems we've done enough sessions now that she's realized no one will stop listening. I don't know how she can remember this, when she can't remember my age or what button to press in the elevator that takes us down to our bunker.

Sometimes I become convinced that Ma's only pretending to forget. I look at her sideways as we watch TV at night and try to glimpse some knowing expression or telltale smirk that will confirm my theory. But her face remains a mask, one of liver spots and loose skin and faint silver hairs that grow in places they should not be growing. For a while I'd pluck them from her ears and cheeks, but she'd yelp and shoot me looks so thoroughly betrayed that I stopped.

Still, each day I wait for her to take her mask off. To peel it from her face, laughing in that mocking but not entirely mean way she once had, making me the butt of the joke. To go back to being the real Ma, Ma who told me I was lucky to be tall, since it made my oversized feet look smaller; who'd wax her brows into graceful arcs each and every week; who, even at seventy, still had perfect copper highlights in her crown; who made the six-hour flight from Singapore to Seoul once a year for the latest injectable skin treatments.

"Why don't we take a break," Ms. Tan says. An assistant steps up to take the helmet of wires and nodes off Ma's head.

"Rubber seeds," Ma says to me. "Rub against the wall, then press against each other's skin, *tsssssssst!* Aiya! Very hot you know! So fun, we can just spend hours like that every day, chasing each other, trying to burn each other's arm. Last time always so fun."

"Fun," I say. I stroke Ma's hair, the bones of her head taut beneath her scalp.

1°21'28.5"N

* * *

I've heard the rubber-seed story many times. It's one of Ma's favorites. I knew the story even before the Remembering began, for it was one she'd tell me at the dinner table in the old times, before the illness hit, on the nights when things were smooth and easy between us. Feeling good, she'd open a bottle of red wine, try to get me to drink even though she knew I'd say no. After the first glass her eyes would grow glassy and she'd begin to reminisce, telling me stories of *before Pa left* and *before Ah Ma died* and *before this or that brother got mad with this or that sister* and everything was the way it should be, everything was better, everyone was happy.

When an old memory is recalled, it retraces the synaptic pathway in which it originated. One would think this makes it stronger, more indelibly real, and yet the very act of recall is one of authorship. Each retracing affects the pathway. And thus a memory is a fragile thing, disintegrating a little more each time it is summoned.

Sometimes I liked listening to Ma. It was seductive, this remembering, a reconstruction of the before to make the after bearable. Other times I got angry, couldn't ignore the way that, each time a story was told, something would be embellished to make it ever simpler and kinder, ever fuller of bullshit love and harmony. "Pa was already gambling when you met him," I'd say. "And Ah Ma had always been bitter that Tai Ma wouldn't let her go to school. She terrorized your sisters, beat them, Ah Ee is always showing me that triangle scar on her shoulder."

When I said these things, we'd fight. By then she'd be on her second drink, maybe the third, and the insults would begin. "You don't know anything, you never even tried to get to know Ah Ma and now she's dead and it's too late, you never even learn Hokkien, how can you say you understand anything at all?" At this point, if I backed down, we'd be okay. The night would settle back into a grudging sort of peace–I contrite, she wronged but magnanimous. But sometimes I didn't want peace, I wanted truth. Or maybe I just wanted the pieces of the world to click into the particular pathways I had assembled, just for once. I wanted to be right. I wanted her to say I was right, and, of course, she never would. Now, she never could.

* * *

"The way the leaves on the trees move," Ma says. "They think they will be here forever is it?"

She's looking out the window. An enormous rain tree, its trunk whole and unblistered, its canopy luxuriant with green, leaves dry and entire, set aglow by the evening sun. There are still trees here, here being the high areas behind the wall. The scene out the window is one that looks little different from what it might have before the water came: tall building upon tall building; trees, large and old, not unlike the rain tree Ma points to; people, everywhere. The trees line the roads, paired neatly with working streetlamps. Overhead, bridges are painted forest green to blend in. We're far enough from the seawall that we can't see its gray, looming bulk. Only the swarms of people and glossy rectangular glass boxes on every block give any hint at all that the world has changed. Elevator stations, guarded by uniformed army boys, marked with the underground sectors they serve. The elevators lead to the residential bunkers that crowd the space beneath the earth, inverted skyscrapers that go thirty, forty floors deep.

They ask for your identification card when you go in. They ask for your identification card when you come out. Exit passes are limited, and even with the system in place, the streets are still overcrowded. Six million people, five and a half million of whom are now housed underground in this meager parcel of dry earth; if everyone were let out at the same time, there would be no place to stand. Yet we are the lucky ones, for at least we live behind the seawall, beyond the reach of the ever-encroaching waves, the famine and disease, the pirate gangs that ply the decommissioned zones.

Still, we cannot help but envy the elite few whose lives continue unchanged, who can afford homes within the last remaining gated enclaves aboveground. Fresh air, the feeling of wind in one's hair, an unfiltered sky; these, like so many other things, have become luxuries afforded only to the wealthy.

Before: it's not as if the city wasn't already packed before the water came.

Singapore, third densest country in the world. Six million on an island thirty-one miles long, seventeen miles wide. Most of us already lived in towers, soaring and densely packed. Back in the old neighborhood, our flat was on the twenty-eighth floor, high above the tops of trees, close enough to the next block to see into our neighbors' kitchens. Now we're on the thirty-fourth floor, only deep beneath the earth. We're closer than ever before to our neighbors, but there are no windows underground, only ventilation grates and concrete walls.

There is a symmetry to our lives, past height mirrored by present depth. The way we live is a daily reminder that for every action, one equal and opposite waits just around the corner.

We tried to stay in the old flat even after the water came, even after our block was decommissioned. Old Mr. and Mrs. Sulaiman stayed, too, along with the spitting ginger cat who always followed them to the coffeeshop, who turned sweeter and needier as the waters rose. The Lee family, with their brood of six children and the noisy canaries they kept in the common corridor, feathers permanently bedraggled from the rain. The young Gupta couple, she pregnant and serene, he perpetually anxious, his cheeks turning hollow as hers filled out.

We thought we could make it work, all of us banding together, taking turns to catch the water taxi out to the few markets that were still operational, bringing back food and supplies each week. When the electricity went out, we switched to candles and kerosene lamps, the Sulaimans remarking that this was no different from how they used to live before they moved from their kampong into the flats. When the taps in our kitchens ran dry, we bought large plastic kegs of distilled water that we installed in the shared corridor, and the Lees said it was like the common tap they'd line up at in the old wooden shophouses.

Time seemed to be moving backward, and this did not feel like an entirely unhappy thing. We'd spent so long worrying about what would happen when the waters came that when they finally did, it was a relief to find ourselves still here. There was a comfort to be had in abstract problems turned concrete, in the hypothetical being made real at last. It narrowed the gaze, turning life into a series of logistical problems that could only be tackled day by day.

How, for instance, one was to keep meat fresh when the refrigerator no longer worked, and afternoons had turned so hot that food would spoil in its packaging on the way home. We designated Wednesday meat day, and whoever was responsible for the shopping that week would go out in the early morning, as the sun's first rays were hitting the pale water and the edges of things were still soft and lined with

1°21'28.5"N

gold. At that time of day, it was cool enough that one could be outside without a sun-blocking umbrella, though dark glasses were encouraged, retina burn being a stealthy and constant threat. We grew accustomed to having our most lavish meals for breakfast–full spreads of pork trotters in dark sauce, chicken thighs fried in prawn paste, cubes of marbled beef stewed soft and sweet and gingery. We gorged ourselves, eating till our bellies ached so we could skip lunch, tolerate plain bread and crackers for dinner. There was no way to keep the food fresh, so we had to eat it all.

When it wasn't Wednesday, we ate soggy vegetables from cans and tepid slop from army ration packets. Then the riverbanks in Malaysia and Thailand burst, the farms shut down, and meat tripled in price. Meat day went from once a week to once every two weeks, then once a month, then never. Next, fresh vegetables grew dear, then even rice was rationed. It was like the war all over again, the Sulaimans said, when the Japanese invaded. Back, back, the waters were pulling us back. The Sulaimans' earliest memories were their parents describing the hollow feeling one had in the stomach after a meal of sweet potatoes in watered-down rice gruel, and it was this memory that made them decide they had had enough. They were the first of our group to leave the old neighborhood, taking up the government's offer of a bunker beneath dry ground, with the promise of steady, subsidized rations.

No such rations were available to citizens who chose to risk their safety in the decommissioned neighborhoods, for these, in the government's eyes, were quickly becoming havens for the desperate and unlawful traveling into the country from the region. We saw no desperates or unlawfuls, only Thai families making homes in abandoned flats, Cambodian children hard at work on the water taxis, Indonesian women with unfaltering smiles selling packets of Milo and bandung door to door. The edges of our country were dissolving, and yet those in power insisted on those divisions like never before.

The Sulaimans left, then the Lees, then the rest of the block, until only us and the Guptas remained. Mrs. Gupta, plagued by nightmares of babies with milky white eyes, was terrified of her child being born underground.

* * *

"That's enough for today," Ms. Tan says when she returns. "We'll call you to arrange our next appointment."

It's the first time they've cut short a session. I don't know what that means, but I know what will happen if they do. I shoot a glance at Ma, still looking out the window at the trees.

"Do you mind if we stay here a while?" I say in a low voice. "And I know you're very busy, you don't have to stay, but maybe—maybe he can stay too."

I point at the assistant by the door, a string bean of a man, pale and tall, with the face of a boy. He looks up from scrolling away on his phone.

"I don't understand," Ms. Tan says. Her smile growing forced, her gaze already skittering out the door.

"She's very sensitive to change," I say. "She doesn't like it when things change. All we need is to stay here. All we need is someone to listen to her, until the allotted time is up."

Ms. Tan's lips contract into a line.

"Please," I say.

Before: in a different time, before the water and the power cuts and the blazing, scorching heat, I asked a doctor what was best for Ma.

She had just started showing early signs of degeneration, and the diagnosis was tentative but likely. He'd said to keep her in a familiar environment, to keep her physically active and mentally engaged. Even then, he warned, the degeneration was inevitable. Most of all I should tell her that I loved her, for what Alzheimer's patients cannot comprehend with their minds, they can feel with their hearts. I did not know how to tell him that we were not a family that said such things, that I did not know what it meant to feel love with one's heart, except through a splinter one either inflicted on or had inflicted on by the other, and its subsequent removal. But the familiar environment, the physical and mental engagement, I could do.

And so we developed a routine in that flat on the twenty-eighth floor. Each day we got up at seven, Ma preparing toast and a half-boiled egg for me that I swallowed after a quick cold shower. She knew how to do it exactly how I liked, so that the golden yolks trembled with a certain precise degree of liquid, so the whites were congealed but still faintly transparent. Into this I'd tip the usual dark soy sauce and white pepper, swirl the whole semi-solid mixture around until it formed a sweet, bracing mouthful, then slurp directly from the shallow bowl. I'd pick out five crosswords for her to do, and she'd list the errands she had planned for the day. When I came home from work she'd have channel 8 on, the opening credits of the latest seven o'clock drama just beginning as I stepped through the door. We'd eat dinner in front of the TV, then she'd show me her completed crosswords, tell me all that she'd done, all the grievances she'd suffered at the hands of impolite store assistants and rude passersby, complain about her knees getting worse. Around nine, after filling in a sudoku together, we'd retire to our respective rooms.

Ma would get ready for bed on her own. She would go to the bank on her own, she would brew an inky herbal broth over a gas-fired stove on her own. The early signs showed, of course, items gone missing, stories repeated, new acquaintances forgotten. But for the most part things were good, things were fine, before the illness got bad.

Before the illness got bad. After Pa left. *Before* Ah Ma died. After Ma's diagnosis. *Before* the bunker. After the water.

Before Ma forgets.

I don't think about what comes after.

"I can stay," the assistant says.

Ms. Tan shoots a violent glance at him, then at her watch. She says we can stay for ten more minutes, but not a moment longer, because the next Rememberer will be there soon.

When she leaves, I get Ma to lie down in the reclining chair, and the assistant wires her into the recording helmet once again. I thank the assistant. His name is Teck, he says with a kind smile. Ma doesn't notice that Teck doesn't turn the machine on and starts talking right away. Being children, Ma says, she and her cousin used to bathe together even though he was a boy, sharing a large bucket of well water between the two of them. They'd draw the water–she stops, frowns.

"How come not working," she says. She shakes her head, squints, then stares at me accusingly. "How come not working!"

I turn to Teck. "Please," I say in a quiet voice. "I won't tell anyone."

Teck's worried eyes widen, his long, pale face seeming to grow paler, longer. He looks at Ma. Her small hands are clenched into fists and she won't stop blinking, pupils twitching from side to side, as if hoping that each blink will reset reality, take her out of this cold, gray room and back into her Rememberings. Teck sighs.

"Just ten minutes," he says, and turns the machine on.

Soon Ma's back amongst the soaring rubber trees, feet trampling through unruly ferns and twisting tree roots, burning seeds clasped hot like beating hearts in the palm of each hand.

The Remembering kicked off around the time we moved underground. A flyer was waiting for us inside our bunker, glossy and trifold, a picture of a gray-haired woman sitting in an armchair, a rapt audience of children at her feet. DO YOU HAVE STORIES TO TELL? the brochure said. WHAT DO *YOU* REMEMBER?

I'd heard about the project, of course. Everyone had. Our final, last-ditch attempt to fix things as a nation. Once it became clear that the water was inevitable, that the biofuels and levees were never going to be enough, the research grew scattered and fantastical, desperate and harebrained. Floating cities, artificial islands, entire countries elevated on stilts. Perhaps it's unfair to call them harebrained, since out of them came the bunkers, and the bunkers saved millions of lives. Situated in the lowest-risk areas of the island–that is, the middle. Farthest from the coast, highest above the sea. A wall was built around the area, a fifteen-kilometer radius, a citadel of dry land, with the unsaid understanding that everything outside of it would eventually be abandoned.

Everything was about the bunkers, and so when the Remembering project was revealed, it came as a surprise to most. The government had been working on it in secret, the brightest minds in the nation harnessed to develop a machine-learning program like no other. The idea was simple. Climate change being too big a problem for the human mind to solve, too complex and multivariate for scientists or politicians to grapple with, the thinking went, salvation could come only from the mind of a machine.

Hence the Remembering: memories gathered from those who still recalled the world as it once was, offered as data points to the program, god of algorithms. All the data was valuable, all of it, for that was the beauty of machine learning. What our limited human minds saw as insignificant could possess great meaning. Answers found in that which our flawed and mortal souls could only perceive as randomness.

Ma picked the flyer up and stared at it for a long time, touching her finger to each of the faces of the children. It had always pained her that I'd never had any, but by this time the disease had advanced enough that she was starting to forget it did.

"I want to do this," she said, and I didn't see why not. It worried me to think of Ma underground all day, without the Guptas to check in on or the tops of trees to look at. We had neighbors here, too, hundreds of them, but everyone kept their doors shut, per the protocol. An open or incorrectly sealed door triggered an alarm that involved a dispatch team and a not insignificant fine for the forgetful bunker-dweller. All this for our own safety–the warren could flood at any time, and our doors were the only things keeping us safe. In any case, no one wanted to linger in those corridors, fluorescent-lit and with the stale smell of recirculated air.

We filled in the forms for Ma to take part. I worried her condition would disqualify her, but she was only required to remember up to 2020–that is to say, around the time the world got bad. It was the last ten years that Ma had trouble with. Her memory seemed to slip away the higher the waters rose.

"Can she remember her childhood?" the woman on the phone asked.

"*Can* she," I said.

It turned out Ma was so good at Remembering that they increased her sessions to twice, then three times a week. At first it was the buildings they were interested in, so Ma regaled them with the particulars of every single home she'd lived in, from the attap house in a kampong that farmed hefty, turgid pigs, to the wooden shophouse with no ceiling, shared with three other noisy families, to the small but shockingly modern one-bedroom flat, with electricity and piped water, this shared with just one other family, to the first home she'd ever had that was truly her own, the larger, even more modern flat she'd moved into after getting married, with its own bathroom and kitchen. Then they wanted to know about the schools she attended, how many students were in each class, what the classrooms looked like, where the teachers went during breaks. Clothing, friends, jobs, what market she bought her fish at, how much she paid for it.

Ma was so good at Remembering that, a few months in, she received a certificate of appreciation, signed by the deputy minister himself, recognizing her for valuable services rendered. I put her in her best dress–a navy cheongsam with silver embroidered flowers that once fit her like a glove, but now hung loose as a shift–and together we attended the prize ceremony. It was ordinary citizens like Ma, they said during the opening speech, who would enable us to overcome these dark times as a nation. Ma didn't like the ceremony. The auditorium was too cold, she said, and the air conditioning made her eyes hurt. She didn't understand why she had to go up on the stage, and thought she had done something wrong that she was being reprimanded for. It was like in secondary-school days, she said, where misbehaving students would be caned publicly on stage. I accepted the certificate on her behalf.

Prize ceremony aside, the Remembering was a miracle for Ma. Her moodiness disappeared, and while she still didn't know certain things like Pa being dead and not just missing, or me being divorced and hence living with her, she stopped, for the most part, asking about them. She took what she didn't know placidly, without overturning bowls of soup or dashing table lamps to the floor, instead merely saying "Oh?" The Remembering sessions calmed her, gave her tumultuous mind peace. Though we dwelled for the most part like moles beneath the earth, she lived, three times a week, in the dry, old world, a world with grass and trees, where family was loving and neighbors were kind, and there was enough food, water, and space for all.

Today, Ma has disappeared. I get home to the bunker at seven in the evening as usual, undo the complex series of locks and seals on the concrete outer door, pass into the safety chamber, then open the inside door–three inches of heavy metal, our last line of defense should everything else fail–only to find the living room empty and silent. No upbeat theme music from the TV, no wafting plastic scent of rations warming on the two-burner stove, no pile of completed crosswords neatly stacked in the center of the coffee table. No Ma. I check the bedroom, the bathroom, but the bunk beds are empty, the toilet unoccupied. There are no other rooms.

I find her, finally, back in the safety chamber. There is a narrow, tall cupboard on the wall between the metal inside door and the concrete outer door, and there Ma is, standing muttering and pale-faced, pressed up against the fuse box and gas pipes.

It's been two weeks, and still I haven't received the call to schedule Ma's next session. I can't figure out what we've done wrong–if it's what happened in the last session, Teck having betrayed us, or if Ma's memories have simply ceased to be useful. Each time I call the Ministry they tell me Ms. Tan isn't available, and that they will call me back when she is.

"Where were you going," I ask, voice steady at first, but then she doesn't answer, only continues muttering, and I shout my question again. "Where did you think you were going?"

"Ms. Lim," she says. "Ms. Lim Hwee Kim, please step on the stage! Careful, careful, ah, wah, so pretty, ravishing, step up, step up, careful! Ladies and gentlemen, Ms. Lim Hwee Kim!"

Is this a memory? I can't tell. She's told me before about being scouted off the street for a Miss Singapore pageant, but I never got the details other than Ah Ma forbidding her to participate once she found out. Is she in a dream, a reverie of what might have been? Or is there more to the story than she's ever told me: did she disobey Ah Ma, sneak out secretly, join the pageant anyway–win, even–and conceal it from everyone her entire life? The last person she'd tell is me, of course. In all her stories to me she is the paragon of filial piety, a perfect, obedient daughter, one I will never live up to.

Ma's disappearance confirms one thing: the illness is getting worse. She's never tried to leave the bunker without me before. It's a third the size of our old flat, but I've crammed in all our furniture, put up our family photos, the tearaway calendar she likes, the round plastic clock with the incredibly loud second hand. It feels enough like home, and for the most part I think she thinks it is. She hasn't questioned the lack of windows or the ventilation hum. The first week after we moved here she asked about the Guptas constantly, but hasn't now, in months. I showed her how the locks and seals on the two doors work, how the second won't open unless the first is closed and so on, but she appeared not to be listening and showed no inclination to go out at all. And so she leaves the bunker only two to three times a week–as many times as there are Rememberings scheduled. At least that's how it's been in the past year that we've lived here, in the past year up till now.

After I get Ma settled in front of the TV, warmed vegetable curry over rice on a tray on her lap, I call the Ministry again. They're closed now, so I leave a long, angry message about social responsibility, simple politeness, and basic competence. How do they expect to reverse time, to reconstruct our world as it was before, if they show such utter disorganization in the simple data-collection phase? "My mother is aged," I say, "and still going out of her way to do a service to the nation. The least the nation could do in return is take our calls."

I feel better after I put down the phone, but the next morning the Ministry calls back to say that Ma's been cut from the program, and that is why no sessions have been arranged. Her service has been very much appreciated, and a certificate of exceptional contribution will be coming by mail within three business days.

I've never Remembered, myself. From what I understand, the wires create the world in the mind's eye of the Rememberer as they speak, plunging them into the reality that they recall into being. It's a sophisticated data-gathering tool, designed to glean input directly from the Rememberer's synapses and then feed the images, sights, and sounds back to them directly so as to stimulate a deeper quality of recollection.

There are things I want to say to Ma that she will not understand now. Things like: I'm sorry I fought you until you couldn't fight anymore. Like: I know now that what I saw as a battle of wills was really a battle of love.

I don't remember what our strife was about anymore. I know the material details: my childhood swinging wildly between extreme strictness and borderline neglect; the occasional, mild acts of violence; her hatred and torment of Chor Seng–*your wastrel husband*, as she called him, as he frustratingly turned out to be. Me running away to a different country, a different life, because I thought that everything she stood for was wrong. I can recite them by heart, these old stories of love and hurt, and yet the more I go over them in my mind, the more they feel like they happened to someone else. They certainly don't feel as dire as I once thought. In fact they are embarrassing, mundane in the cold light of passed time. Where the anger used to dwell in me there is nothing but a dent–smooth, hollow, soft darkness pooled under the awning of a bruised collarbone.

Today I come home to silence again, no synthesized TV violin when the concrete outer door thuds open. In the safety chamber, I check the utility closet before even going into the bunker–I've found her there three times now in the past week alone—but it is empty except for a tangle of wires, no Ma. I unlock the metal inner door with dread in my stomach, knowing that this is yet another new low, another thing to get used to. Finding her in the utility closet has become its own routine in the past month, since the Remembering sessions have stopped, a new normal to which we have both become accustomed. But now—no TV, no closet.

The metal door swings open and I see why the TV isn't on. It's on the floor, broken glass strewn over the concrete, catching the fluorescent light in a cruel way. The coffee table's been tipped over, too, cushions from the sofa ripped and oozing stuffing. All the pictures have been pulled off the wall. It looks like a crime scene, but in the middle of it all is Ma, sitting on the floor, cradling air in her hands. She's shaking, her bone-thin arms trembling in the girlish off-shoulder blouse she picked out this morning. When she looks up at me, eyes red-rimmed and feral, my heart squeezes so hard I too want to smash everything that hasn't already been broken.

Instead I go to her, press my body to her side, wrap my arms around her cold, thin form. I feel the knobs of her elbows dig into my side, smell the familiar papery salt of her hair, rest my forehead against her cheek. She places a hand on the back of my head, and my eyes grow hot. I know I'm meant to be comforting her, but I can't help feeling like I am the child. Which, of course, I am.

"How come here got no windows?" Ma says. "What happen to our flat? Where are the windows? Where is Mrs. Gupta? She give birth already? I thought I was dying. Like nightmare like that. Cannot breathe. I thought you left me here to die."

I squeeze her tighter. How to explain that we're thirty floors beneath the earth, how to say that our flat might be underwater by now, that I have no idea where the Guptas are or what happened to them but in all likelihood, if they stayed put, they have either starved or drowned to death.

"I won't leave you," I say instead. "I'll never leave you."

"I want to go home," Ma says.

"We are home. This is home. Look!" I say, pointing to the uncomfortable rattan couch she bought for our flat three decades ago, the knickknacks gathered on trips to Australia, little ceramic owls with yellow eyes and cheerful gnomes in old-timey overalls. Hanging by the door: the wooden sign with ugly purple flowers weaving their way around the word HOME.

   "I want to go home," Ma says. "I want to go home, I want to go home, I want to go home."

I take a leave of absence from my job at the textile distribution firm. They'll keep the position for me for a week, but beyond that no promises can be made. "It's the way things are now," my supervisor says apologetically. "You understand."

   I do. Nine job-seekers to every vacant position, record unemployment, entire industries brought to their knees by current conditions–I've seen the headlines, over and over. The only positions really open these days are in engineering and crisis response, and neither are skills I possess. Besides, I don't want a job that has anything to do with the water.

   I call the Ministry again and again. At first they put me on hold repeatedly, then the line begins clicking off after just one ring. I try calling at different times of day, early morning, mid-afternoon, evening, middle of the night. All to the same result.

   After Ma's episode, I put the living room back in order, throwing out the trashed television and torn cushions, sweeping the broken glass into a paper bag that's sitting by the door now, the only remaining sign of her outburst. But something's changed. Ma won't do her crosswords anymore, only stares at them blankly when I put them in her lap. It doesn't even work when I half-fill them with the wrong words; normally she'd be jumping at the opportunity to correct me, to show me how it's done, but now all she does is color the squares in till the pencil lead's down to a nub.

I put in a request for a secondhand bike helmet and electrical wires. They're delivered with our next batch of weekly rations. It's a child's helmet, bright pink with glittery stars printed on its plastic shell, but it will do all the same. I attach the wires to its base and twist them into a crude simulation of the device Teck put on Ma at each Remembering session. Ma lies down in the tatty old recliner in our living room and I place the helmet over her head, taping the loose end of each wire to her cheek and jaw.

   "Tell me about your cousin Ah Eng," I say. "Where did he live? What did you do when you visited him?"

Ma's face lights up. "Ah Eng," she says. "Ah Eng live near the temple, Telok Ayer there, very busy you know, a lot of people–"

She stops, frowns. "How come not working?"

"It's working," I say. "Ah Eng lives near the temple, where Chinatown is today, right? Above the medicine shop, where he worked with his father?"

Ma's shaking her head. "Not working," she says. "You think I stupid?"

"Tell me about Ah Eng," I say, and tears spill down my cheeks. "At least try. You're not even trying."

Ma's still now, and I can't read her face. Her eyes have a hard, flinty look to them, her mouth a small, wretched knot of flesh. She turns to me. The glitter on the helmet flashes prettily under the fluorescent light, the pink stars are silly and sad, her hair's caught in the tape. I want to take the whole ridiculous contraption off.

"When you were a baby," she says. "You never cry. Such a good girl, we can bring you everywhere, your Pa and I. Go to restaurant, go walk at the beach, just bring you in the pram. You just lie there, always smiling, eating your hands, saliva everywhere. Everyone say you so good. The best baby. Best daughter."

It's the first time in a long, long time that Ma's remembered anything from my childhood. Suddenly I notice that the ceiling, the walls, the floor are all the same seamless gray, that, depending on how the light hits, it is hard to tell where one plane begins and another ends. Or how large or small the room we're in really is. I suddenly become aware of how far from the surface of the earth we are. Safe from the water, yes, but also from the light of the sun, the touch of the wind.

And yet we are the lucky ones. Every day, there are stories of the wretched souls crowding the decommissioned zones outside the seawalls, horrific stories of plundered water taxis, ruthless pirate gangs, squatters crushed under the weight of wet, crumbling buildings. Every day, the news reminds us how lucky we are to be alive. And yet.

"Why don't you get dressed, Ma," I say. "Let's go out."

She blinks, and the sad, knowing look falls from her face.

"Go where," she says, and she is an old, tired owl once again, resigned and confused.

"The Ministry. We have a session, remember?"

She frowns but allows me to take the bike helmet off and goes to get dressed. While she's gone, I call the Ministry again. It rings twice, then goes to the automated message I've heard countless times now. The Ministry values your call and we regret that we are presently unable to attend to you. Please try again later.

Ma appears, a vision in yellow. She has on a bright linen top she used to only wear on holiday, a maroon brooch in the shape of a bee, cobalt slacks. She's combed her thin, shoulder-length hair with a little water, and her lips are dabbed with her favorite mauve lipstick. She's smiling. She looks better than she has in weeks.

"Let's go," I say. As we leave, I grab the paper bag containing the broken TV glass. It clinks delicately, a wind chime in a windless place. I remember picking the shards from the floor the night before, weighing each in the palm of my hand, testing their pointed edges with the soft pads of my fingertips.

Here we are in the hallway, long, airless, and bright. Here we are in the elevator lobby, scanning our identity cards in the reader. Here is the elevator. B34. Two people already inside, sallow strangers who nod and look away. Here we step in. Despite the elevator's sleek glass and metal, the smell of dust and damp only intensifies. Here we go, up and up, Ma clinging to the banister pale-faced as if she hasn't been in here hundreds of times before. Here I am, comforting her with one hand, holding the bag of glass in the other. We passed the rubbish chute on the way to the elevator lobby and I did not stop. Here I am, thinking about the possibilities for all this glass.

The light changes, growing warm and soft. The ache inside me is a bruise being pressed. When the elevator doors open, it is almost too much to bear. The smell of dust and damp turns to salt laced with the sweetness of trees, the acrid smoke of cars. The ventilation hum gives way to the pliant cries of oriole birds and the quiet lapping of distant waves everywhere. The wind and sun touch my skin, and I can taste the late morning on the tip of my tongue.

"IC," the army boy at the elevator station says. "Purpose of exit?"

I hand over our identity cards. "Recreational," I say.

He beeps them with his hand scanner and reads the screen.

"Please note you only have two recreational exits left for the month," he says. "Any other exits will have to be applied and paid for three days in advance."

I thank him and we leave. Ma asks why I used a recreational pass when we get free exit passes from the Ministry for Rememberings, but I distract her with a question about the umbrellas, which we have forgotten. It's only a short walk to the bus, and we both have SPF 70+ on, so we keep going.

I walk slowly. Each step is a sensory overload, the dry, clean pavement beneath our feet a miracle to behold. The broad raintrees that line the roads tower overhead, their rustling canopies glowing with light. Cars pass by, government vehicles or private ones belonging to the extremely wealthy who maintain residences aboveground at exorbitant cost. We pass one such complex, a collection of slate towers with vertical gardens spilling down their sides, armed guards flanking trickling fountains at their high iron gates.

We're waiting for the bus, and then we're on it. I marvel at the ordinariness of the morning, the people pressed tight around us in shoes and pants and dresses, all going places of their own. You can tell who lives aboveground by who is on their phone and who isn't. I recognize those on exit passes. Like me, their faces are filled with greed, straining with hunger for the sunlit world. Our eyes dart from outside to inside to outside again, linger on the faces of strangers, skitter across the landscape feverishly. You can almost see our ears pricked, our nostrils flared. Our spit-slick mouths hang just slightly open.

Ma and I disembark in front of the Ministry. The entrance, a set of tall glass doors that open into an expansive lobby, is usually crowded with silver-haired Rememberers and their relatives or case managers, men and women upright or with canes, bright- or cloudy-eyed. It's usually a fight to get in line to check in. But today the lobby is mostly empty as we step inside, with only a few Rememberers sitting on plush sofas in the waiting area.

"How can I help you?" the receptionist asks.

"Checking in Ms. Lim Hwee Kim," I say.

My skin is sensitive, raw, like I've been out in the sun too long, and perhaps I have. It is as if I can feel every single hair on my skin moving in its follicle, as if each follicle is connected directly to my brain. Every light breeze, every accidental jostle amplified and overwhelming.

The woman types, stares at the screen, types again, stares.

"I'm sorry. We don't have her in the system," she says. "You must be mistaken."

I think of our home. Our old home, my childhood home, the breezy flat on the twenty-eighth floor, out in the decommissioned zone. The living room, where we watched soaps and variety shows together each night. The kitchen where Ma made pork trotters so soft they melted on your tongue, cubes of chicken crackling with sweet sesame glaze. Ma's bedroom, where as a girl I'd stumble in the middle of the night when woken by a nightmare. Crawl into the warm nest that smelled of her, a smell I could disappear into, a smell that did not end where I began. Those rooms are empty now. Waterlogged and rotting, sinking into the sea.

"Why?" Ma says. "What's wrong?"

"Nothing's wrong," I say. I ask the woman to check again.

I know we don't have an appointment. I know Ma's not in there, not anymore. I just want to be here a little longer. To stand in this lobby with a sense of purpose, to participate in the world in some insignificant but visible way. I want the receptionist to enter Ma's name into the search function of her database again and again. I want the cameras overhead to record our presence, to have a security officer in some darkened room somewhere see our figures flit across the grainy screens.

I'm lying, that's not all I want. I want our lives back. I want our world back, dry and whole, unblistered and perfect, the way things were before. Before, before, before. I don't need you to tell me these are impossible things.

Not for Ma, though.

Ma can Remember. She can have her childhood again, her cousins, the thick undergrowth and soaring rubber trees. I can't go back in time, I can't be the best daughter, but I can give her this.

The paper bag is heavy in my left hand. It clinks as I reach into it, touch the cold, smooth chunks. A jagged edge scratches my palm, and the pain is both a reminder and a promise. I test each piece, picking them up, putting them down, feeling their shapes with the tips of my fingers. Eventually I find one that will do: a little larger than my hand, elongated with a sharp, eager tip. I take it out, step behind the receptionist's desk. The Rememberers on the sofa are drowsing. No one else is in line. Only Ma sees me grab the receptionist's arm, press the glass to her wrist.

"Check again," I say.

DRONES ABOVE
THE CORAL SAND
by Claire G. Coleman

I'M STANDING ON ONE OF the whitest beaches in the world, or at least that is what I am told. I know from this that I can trust nothing I hear. In reality it's a faint cream-gray, barely blinding, a hurtful, spiteful off-white, like an ancient limestone road, like a marble wall; only the shadows where my feet have dug in as I walked offer any relief to the eyes at all. It is far from enough.

Down at my bare feet the truth is revealed: this beach is not quite white, it's a rainbow, a scattering, a flicker of colored light, dead creatures, lost shells, lives no longer being lived. Every broken shell is a source of mourning, a rebuke, a tear from the depths of the ocean. Broken dead coral, cracked scattered shells, have long ago overwhelmed and covered the sand.

I can hear the insect whine of a distant drone, surely a warning. Proper drones, surveillance drones, would be far too high for me to hear; or they would be silent, near invisible, floating on gossamer solar-plastic wings, lifted aloft by their breath. Either someone unofficial is watching me or someone official wants to be certain I know I am being watched. Or they desire to see how I will react; to see how much I fear their surveillance.

If I run they will know I fear them; if I don't they might suspect I know they are trying to scare me.

I cannot risk raising a camera, taking an obvious photo. I cannot risk launching the drone in my backpack. I cannot suddenly walk away, making it clear I was up to what the drone controllers would define as "no good."

All I can do is stand there, on the cream-gray dead-shell-and-coral beach, staring into the distant ocean, listening to the thunder and crash of waves. Or at least give that pretense. I have to hope that the cameras in my earrings, illegal, custom-made, expensive—not even mine—are getting the shots I need and streaming them through my phone. Where they go after that, I don't really care. I turn, trying to look just like someone scanning the horizon for hope itself, sweep back my hair from my ears, take a deep breath, and sit down, the broken ghosts of coral digging sharply into my arse through my too-thin clothing.

There's a large, mostly intact piece of coral not far away—rough, forked, the color of bone. I pick it up, turn it over in my hands, heft the weight of it, of the many thousands of tiny lives that created it, died creating it. I can feel the age of the reef, like holding a dinosaur bone. I ponder how long it washed in the waves before striking the beach. It can't have been long; the sand in the waves would have ground it to nubbins, smoothed off the tiny jags where the coral had lived. Maybe it was only in the waves for a few days, a few weeks; it might have broken free recently, might have been living only months ago.

I take off my backpack, unzip it, unroll an ancient reusable grocery bag, wrap the coral in it, and slide it carefully into my backpack, beside my drone.

My sweat, from fear and the oppressive wet heat, sticks my pants to my legs, dampens the debris and coral under my thighs. I shouldn't be out here, not on such a hot day. I am too obviously endangering myself, a serious tactical error. I could have no real excuse for being out here, it's too hot standing on the beach, it's too dangerous to swim; tiger sharks compete with crocodiles to eat anyone foolish enough to enter the water. I stand, slip on my backpack, bounce on the balls of my feet to settle the weight, turn my back to the water, and walk.

The first building I come across is too damaged to use. The king tides, the storms, rising seawater and neglect, have torn the ocean-side facade off; coral sand has filled the lower levels, washed in by waves, blown in by wind. I cannot tell if it is genuinely on the verge of falling, its foundation undercut by the wash, by the storms; perhaps it's just my imagination. I skirt around the mounds of white sand, past the fallen debris, toward the tidal swamp where a road used to be; where I was told people once promenaded down sidewalks under the palms that are now nothing more than stumps poking jauntily out of salty mud.

I can no longer hear the drone that has been following me at a distance, although I don't recall when the sound disappeared. I am nowhere near stupid enough to believe that there is nobody and nothing watching me. Something sparkles above me and to the right, among the vines cascading from ruined balconies that clutch the side of the jauntily leaning building. It could be a drone, silent and parked, gripping the strangling vines with plastic claws, watching me; it could be the glass in an intact window, if such a thing still exists in this ruined, abandoned town.

The swamp, formed by floodwater, rising tides, and storms, is silent in the heat, but for the buzz of mosquitoes, too much like the sound of drones to allow me to be comfortable. I don't truly fear the sound—my mind is able to perfectly distinguish bugs from machines—but I am aware that in the sound of the mozzies a drone can hide. Even the warning sound of the drones sent only to tell us somebody is watching will disappear in the buzz.

I have heard rumors of them deploying swarms of drones, each the size of an insect; electronic creatures, with hive minds, by the thousands.

If that is true, if such things exist, why am I still free?

My home—well, the home I am forced to share with many others—tramps, thieves, outlaws, and vagabonds—is an intact but officially abandoned hotel on a low island of briny mud. It sits in a swamp scattered with the corpses of edifices that have not survived. As I approach I can hear the sound of children and can smell cooking. I wonder where someone found food worth cooking, more exciting than the protein pastes and canned shit we have all been living on. I know people have been fishing, there are always people fishing, but in the open sea, no longer protected by the reef, there are no fish to catch. There's a haze of campfire smoke, much of it originating from a gap where a windowpane used to be. The mozzies, as if intuiting that their slim chance to feed on my blood will soon be gone, are dive-bombing me despite the stench of the synthetic citronella oil on my skin.

The doors on the ocean side have long ago disappeared behind a wall of sand-bags higher than me–the bags had been buried in sand drifts even before I first found the place–so I splash ankle-deep down the long, insect-infested path to what would have been the back door when the building was a hotel, when people still came here for holidays to see the reef. I have only vague memories of hearing about that.

The reef once defended this coast from the waves, but no longer. Waves were battering the coast flat, eating the few buildings that had not submerged under the rising sea, that had not sunk into softening sand and fallen. The same heat that has made the sea rise, that is making sweat bead on my skin, that is giving mosquitoes courage, is killing what is left of the reef.

I reach where the inland-facing doors used to be when there was a road, when there were doors; when there was a reef and a reason to visit. It's better, cooler, in the shade, under a roof, where once cars dropped people off when there were people visiting the hotel, when people could still own cars. I can't see into the door-way through the darkness as thick as a curtain, but I know I am being watched. It is not the cold, clinical watching of a drone or a camera. I can almost feel the direct pressure of human eyes upon my skin.

I step through the door–a leap of faith into pitch black, at least until my eyes adjust. There's no sudden sensation of a shiv in my gut so I know I must have been recognized, although I don't remember the face of the person who stands there, borderline threateningly, as I brush past them. Past the entrance is a sunken lobby, genuinely sunken. Once the sea levels rose, it became a pool, saltwater and salt mud, stinking and full of rot and drifting biomass; full also with trash and debris, the detritus of a hundred or so people living what small lives they could.

Long ago someone, perhaps overtaken by a morbid mood, stood a huge piece of dead coral in the middle of the pool, its broken forks reaching into the darkness like skeletal fingers. I hate it, it makes me sick, but I am too disgusted and scared to wade into the pool to remove it.

The bottom dozen steps leading out of the lobby are water-damaged, wood-worm-eaten, and salt-encrusted. It's a little scary climbing over them. I grip the banister hard until I am standing on something more solid. I have a long way to go and the elevator in this building has been rusted out of operation since long before I came here. I have protection, powerful friends–or, more accurately, people with power here owe favors to my powerful friends elsewhere–which is why I live on the second floor from the top, far from the floods and more crowded lower levels. Closer to the smoke that wends its way up the stairwells and through the cracks, settling just below the roof.

The most important thing about being near the top: I have a few minutes longer to react to a raid if one happens. Not if–when. Raids always happen; the fun is in predicting which agency will arrive first and then call in the others because, let's face it, government agencies and the agents of private enterprise love sharing information.

My door is closed, which is good. The hair I stuck with spit across the narrow gap between the door and the frame is still there, and my key turns in the old-fashioned barrel lock convincingly. I walk in. My room is undisturbed.

It's minimally furnished, if you could call it furnished at all, a blank canvas of a room, unless the growing mold stains on the walls count as decoration. Most of the wood within–furniture, wardrobe doors, the kitchen cupboards–was torn out long ago and presumably used as firewood. On the only shelf on the wall, a piece of rough board someone before me attached using bent metal and nails, are my treasures–pieces of dead coral, brightly colored shells, a shark tooth.

In the corner is another pile of coral, pieces rejected as I find new ones and, if they are better, replace the least beautiful. I pull the chunk of coral out of my back-pack and place it on the shelf, displacing another piece to the pile.

On the wall beside my bed there's a bright glossy photo of coral, blue water, and fish. I know why it's there, right there; it's to hide, to help me forget the bullet hole in the wall, haloed with droplets of dried blood. I don't know whose blood, I will never know, I don't want to know. Next to the bed, curling from the damp air, is a colorful children's book about the reef: a reminder, an accusation.

The bedroll, made of seaweed packed in a stitched-together nylon tarpaulin, shaggy where the nylon is deteriorating, and the plaid plastic bag with the rest of my stuff in it are the only other things I have added to the emptiness. Everything is expendable, as am I.

The bathroom: a stained dry bathtub, a completely dry toilet bowl, a tiny window to the outside that is so gray and mucky barely any light pokes through. I force the jammed glass open and take a camouflage cloth sack out of my backpack. I put my backpack into the sack, pull the drawstring closed, reach through the window, and hook a carabiner on a protrusion on the outside wall among the vines. I slide my backpack out the window, knowing not only that it will be invisible from outside, but also that unless someone knows where to put their hand to grab it, they will never find it.

I close the window.

I wash my face with some of the rainwater I keep in a bucket in the bathroom and slip back into my room.

The sun is not coming in through the glass door to my balcony yet but when I look out, the balcony itself is in full scorching daylight. I close a tattered curtain over the window, strip off my clothes, and lie down on my bedroll naked. It's sticky and scratchy; it crackles when I move. I close my eyes so I can't see the sweat beading on my skin. I try to imagine what this room would have felt like with air conditioning, before the collapse, before this town was all but abandoned. I hope that such imagining will cool me as I attempt to sleep.

It's too hot. I take out my phone and watch the news. Nothing new, as always. Sweeping new powers for the police and other government agencies to protect the environment, to investigate environmental crimes, to protect corporations from protest, and to stop anyone from restricting the flow of electricity; and no discussion on how those things are contradictory. Calls again to return to democracy; photos of protesters being teargassed, refugees being detained, brown women in jail, refugees dying of despair in detention.

More fear, more police powers; food riots and freedom protesters being shot in the streets; soldiers in the streets. Racism, more racism. The environmental crisis has made some white people desperate to create white homelands in places where there had never been one, to save what can be saved for them and theirs only.

I wish I could open the window, let in the breeze, but the wind at this time of the day is too hot; it would not cool my skin. The room breathes with moisture; the rising damp from the swamp and the near 100 percent humidity won't let the sweat evaporate. Sleep and dreams don't come, only heat.

Upstairs, sent there by a cryptic message on my phone; the man in the penthouse could have come from anywhere. His features are from everywhere and nowhere at once.

"Do you have everything you need?" His voice is so deep I can feel it in my gut, like being hugged.

I nod. His penthouse has actual furniture: an ugly, scratched brown leather couch; a messy bed; cupboards. It is nevertheless stark. Not the emptiness that comes from having nothing, but the emptiness that comes from being selective. The only decoration is an Aboriginal flag hanging on the wall.

"I'm okay," I breathe finally. "Thank you for keeping an eye on me and my stuff, for the room."

He waves that away like someone shooing flies. "The people you are working for, I owe them more than I would like to admit. Keeping an eye on you, giving you a home here, that's only a little thing." He crosses the room and I am staring at the silhouette he creates in the glazed window. It's cooler up here than I had thought it would be, but there's even more smoke settling here than in my room, the walls are yellow with it, it hazes the air and catches in my lungs.

"Besides," he continues, "you and your people are a thorn in the side of E & E; the eco-fascists hate you with a fierce will, fierce enough to make them crazy, make them stupid. I find that quite endearing."

I shudder, gall floods my mouth, I can feel the fear in my gut. "What if they come for me, what if they raid this place? I will put you and all the people living here in danger." I punctuate the sentence with a cough.

The silhouette in the window shrugs. "They are always coming for somebody, they are always raiding for some reason, we are always in danger. Most of the people living here have been in trouble since before they came here; the children," he pauses for a breath, "the children were in danger before they were born. What you are doing, proving the damage is still happening to the reef, it is not a small thing. If you need anything, let me know."

"I will," I lie. I leave the penthouse and descend the frighteningly rickety stairs. I check that nobody has invaded my crappy empty room while I was gone, climb onto my damp mattress, and try to sleep.

The falling sun is throwing my shadow into the waves where once, I am assured, a lagoon used to be; or perhaps my shadow has not even reached the edge of the pre-rise ocean; I don't know how far the coastline has moved. I can feel the waning sun heating the back of my neck. It's uncomfortable, crinkling my skin in preparation for blisters.

There could be ships in the distance, out of sight, where the reef used to be. I take out my phone and tap an app icon. The screen goes green, stays green: as safe as it's going to be. I drop to my knees, ignoring the poke and scrape of shells and coral, and pull a rolled-up beach blanket out of my bag. Unrolling it I catch the folded drone before it tumbles out onto the ground. Loading another app, I unfold and launch my drone, watching from my knees, embedded in the sand and bones of coral, as it flies out into the distance.

I pray I have programmed it properly; I pray it was built to spec; I pray I do not lose the data connection, split and encrypted as it is for safety. I don't even know who I am sending my prayers to.

Not knowing if anyone is watching, I sit back on the blanket and take out a banana. Let it look like a furtive meal, sneaking away from humbuggers, thieves, and muggers to eat a priceless piece of forbidden fruit. I know bananas are illegal, but the crime of eating a banana is less than growing them and far less than launching that drone in the direction I have sent it. I hope nobody watching by high drone will question why I am hiding on a beach. I hope nobody will come, break my solitude, throw me in a prison.

My drone, mostly autonomous, has buzzed out of sight.

I lie back on my ragged, dirty beach towel; my phone, hopefully, is doing its job, the machine-learning algorithm leading the drone where it needs to be, guiding the camera. It's not my job to analyze what the drone discovers—not this time, anyway. I am too exposed to be allowed to know anything; my decision. I didn't want to know where that data was going or what was discovered. Not yet.

Back at base in Brisbane, I assume someone is watching the drone footage. They are presumably watching me, too; I would be if I were them. We are environmentalists, so deep green we border on black. To certain members of the government we are terrorists; I guess they would call me a spy.

My phone beeps; my heart jumps at the sound. It's not a good sound, not a happy sound. I almost sit up in panic, but I control myself; even a high drone at a distance would notice such a human movement and investigate. My hand finds my bag, slips in, and grips my phone. I slide it out as I roll over in the same movement, and the phone ends up almost under my cheek. If I keep my left eye closed I can just barely read the screen. DRONE DOWN.

At the distance it was from me it would have landed in the water, irretrievable. I tap with my finger: the map shows where the drone signal ceased, right where the reef used to be; it is still marked even though it has been dying or near-dead since before I was born. I imagine my drone lurching up and down on waves formed by the slight break, the dead coral. I wonder, then, what could have killed it—battery failure, software crash, a fouled propeller, a drone fence, a well-aimed rifle, interference, an electromagnetic pulse. The app gives me no clue.

I lie back, aware that getting up and running would indicate I had something to do with that drone, assuming it was taken down or destroyed on purpose. The barely-there noise of a drone is in the distance, so far away that the sound comes and goes, so distant I cannot be certain it is intended to be heard.

MCS58

19°41'05.0"S

No time to run; I cannot be seen showing too much fear. I start to slide my phone back into my flaccid backpack, its emptiness reminding me of the missing drone. With that machine gone I have only a short time before I will have to smuggle myself back to the capital, back to Brisbane. My mission was a failure—or perhaps, depending upon what happened to my drone, a roaring success.

The phone vibrates in my hand before I have it concealed. I decide, despite the danger, to look at what it wants. There is a message from a number listed as Ogilvy, one of the numbers pre-programmed on my phone when it was handed to me about a year ago. "Your drone was shot down," the message says. "Get out of there, now."

I take what I think is a short moment to prepare myself. I don't want to look scared when I run. My phone vibrates again. "Why are you not running?" asks Ogilvy.

Surging to my feet, now in a panic, I leave everything on the beach except my empty bag and the phone in my hand and run.

My feet dig into the sand, slowing me down. I left my shoes behind with my towel, but in such a desperate situation it was probably a good idea. Shoes would just make it even harder to run. Behind me is the sound of drone wings, some flapping, some buzzing, others silent, lofted on solar-powered air. I don't know if I can outrun the buzzing, flapping things behind me, and then I hear a louder noise, like a troop-carrier quadcopter in the air before me, thankfully far away, past the edifice in the swamp where I have been living.

The rotted, cracked, salt-gray wood of the old boardwalk over the swamp thunders under my feet, then it runs out. I splat through mud, stumble, almost fall. I reach the road and my feet flap on the concrete roadway, which sits under an inch of water. I don't quite make it to the darkened door before the first drone passes over; I hear its engines just stop, or more accurately I suddenly can't hear them. I hear the drone splat, splash, and clatter into the water atop the roadway. Somebody has deployed a drone fence; somebody fears the drones as much as I do, or they work for the same people I do and want to give me a fighting chance.

Other drones peel away from the pulsing electromagnetic interference that could scramble them, crash them. For now. Soon they will test the fence, find out if any of them have hardened-enough hardware, updated-enough firmware to penetrate a fence that is probably older and less advanced than they are. And there is still the quadcopter, coming in fast and hot; the fence might take it down, too, but that is uncertain and also no help. It could land outside the fence; the troops it is carrying could walk the rest of the way.

I reach the door of my building just before the quadcopter lands. Diving through, I jump to the side and the shiv barely touches my skin. "I live here, dickhead," I shout, already running for the stairs. "Hostiles coming, sound the alarm." I don't slow down to find out if the guard has listened.

Halfway up the stairs my phone beeps, then starts screaming. The alarm app plays an old-fashioned siren sound until I poke the icon and turn it off. I guess someone sounded the alarm.

Stopping at a window that once lit the stairwell before vines overtook it, I look out. Fascist bullyboys in black jumpsuits, four of them, are walking toward the door, armed but showing restraint and, surprisingly, caution. A rock exits the building somewhere above me in a shower of glass and lands on the windshield of the copter, which splashes into glittering fragments.

I start running up the stairs, faint with the exertion and the heat.

I can hear more copters, flocks of drones, boots splatting in the mud.

"They've traced your phone," the voice on the other end says. "I'm not surprised, you got the best footage of the dying reef we have ever seen. We can use it, all of it. The public will know that the restrictions they placed upon us didn't really protect the reef–they were never about protecting the reef."

"Great," I say. "I know filming the reef is illegal but that doesn't explain why they're coming for me so hard." I talk as fast as I can as I run up the stairs.

"There's something else," says Moreau, "something we suspected but never thought we would see: a freighter carrying coal through a hole in the reef. We don't know when they blasted it, but they did. We can see the damage they made clearly in your footage."

"Fuck." I can think of nothing else to say.

"They don't know you were streaming it to us, at least that's what we think. They think you have the footage only on your phone. Get rid of it and get the hell out of there. See you in Brisbane."

I consider my options as I spray out a string of expletives even my friends would be surprised I know. Upstairs, they know I'm not just a random vagabond. Somebody was paying them to protect me, but that protection could evaporate the moment the soldiers come in. The man upstairs might not be willing to help me now that there are actual troops coming. There might be other help I could call on, people working for my people, people working for other allied groups, but I have no idea who they are. I can think of no choice.

I run to a west-facing window. A black all-wheel drive van with the logo of the Department of the Environment and Energy on the side is pulling up. I watch as soldiers in black jumpsuits pour out, eight or twelve, then another van comes. I can see another in the distance, mud and water fan-tailing off its wheels.

Back in my room, I scan my belongings, trying to imagine what I don't want to part with: the twenty-year-old digital camera, a kid's book on the life of the Great Barrier Reef—it was that book that led me to the people I work for—my favorite piece of coral, a bit heavy but I'm not leaving without it. I stick my favorite things in the scrappy old backpack that once held my now-dead drone and run to the window of my room. It faces north.

Reaching back as much as I can, I throw my phone out the window; I don't even watch how far it flies. Turning, I smash out my door, cross the hallway, and kick open a door to a south-facing room. I step through and slam it shut. Someone is home. They look startled and I don't know them.

"Raid," I say, "coming through."

"You can't just—" they start to shout, obviously new here, and I shoulder them out of the way before they finish the sentence. I run to the window, swing out, and lower myself down the trellis.

I have to think fast and move faster. I have to keep moving as I think. I can hear the E & E agents moving up the building; I can hear stuff breaking, unsure whether it's the agents searching for stuff or the residents hiding what they can. There's an abrupt crack and a phone flickers past my face so close I can almost read the screen. The agents are close.

I climb faster.

One floor from the ground I hear a shout: someone has stuck their head out the window; they are shouting and pointing at me. I kick off from the vines I am holding and reach air for a moment, landing in the swamp with a splat.

It takes me only a moment to regain my feet, although my ankle is sore and I am staggering. It's a long way to Brisbane. I can't rely on any help. E & E are looking for me. There's a shout behind me; there are flocks of drones all around me; I start to run.

THE
NIGHT DRINKER
by Luis Alberto Urrea

A CHRONICLE OF THE LAST DAYS OF TENOCHTITLAN,
BUILT ON LAKE TEXCOCO, KNOWN NOW AS MEXICO CITY,
HOME OF THE ANCIENT GODS. 2040 A.D.

(FROM THE NOTEBOOKS OF JOAQUIN HERNANDEZ III, HISTORIAN.
FOUND IN THE RUINS OF IZTAPALAPA, 2045.)

IN THOSE YEARS, THE ONE World, Ce Anahuac as the Aztecs called it, was dying of fever. The world was so hot that monarch butterflies easily caught fire in our mountains. Once the whales died, the oceans crawled onto the shore faster than the scientists had predicted. They came ashore like insidious, living beings, filling the lowlands and drowning the ports. Many crops perished down below; the Mexican plateau around us was safe from ocean flood, but not from drought. The sea was a taunt from the earth–those thirsty people and animals were given water that could not be drunk, and in that tide came garbage and dead creatures and black waves. Mazatlán and Vallarta and Cozumel and Acapulco grew beards of bleached seaweed and battlements of ghostly fishing boats and sideways cruise ships now populated by shrieking coastal birds and starving sea lions. The agua negra poisoned aquifers, as if punishing the land for its sins. Soon, the salted tides corrupted hydroelectric plants and caused blackouts all over the country. Here in La Capital, as my genera-tion still called it, we had wind generators, solar panels, and smart roofs that used greenery, filters, and rain collection to try to clear the air.

The catastrophes in the lowlands panicked the refugees into moving farther and faster than they had moved before, but they were greeted in every territory by walkers fleeing toward the places they'd left. We could not help but be amused when the throngs of gringos rushed the border heading for Chihuahua and Sonora. But who could judge them? The far American West was in ruins. Earthquakes fractured the land, drought killed the crops and turned the hills into tinder, the unexpected monsoons eroded the denuded hills onto the ruins. The Sea of Cortez crept up the dry bed of the Colorado River, then jumped its banks and made a swollen dead sea that poisoned Yuma and Mexicali and Calexico. Those of us with dark senses of humor, and what Mexican does not have a dark sense of humor, found it amusing that the parts of the great border wall still above water were used to tie off the boats of floating scavengers and the undocumented.

Canada finally closed its own borders and used its military to keep Americans from invading. They could not stop the heat, though, or the subsequent spread of tree borer beetles, and the great pine forest fires of 2030 gave them a gray desert north of Minnesota.

The refugees turned to the highlands. San Miguel de Allende, that great Disneylandia of art and crystals and movie stars and peace, already gentrified long ago by expats to the point of pushing local people to the outskirts, began to see walkers from Brazil and Haiti and Honduras and Salvador and even Eritrea, who were climbing up through Guanajuato and Guadalajara on their long journeys to find higher ground. Drought and tides and despair pushed the people. And the refugees rose up the mountains, searching for sanctuary. People thought they were safe in San Miguel, but they weren't.

I, like my grandfather before me, have long been a lover of North American literature, and the writers were always there in San Miguel. I enjoyed San Miguel for many reasons, but Jack Kerouac and Neal Cassady were my chosen ghosts, as I liked to say. I knew which wooden stools in the La Cucaracha bar they had sat on in 1969. I knew the exact bend in the rail line where Cassady lay down and died on a cold night. When San Miguel was overrun, those barstools were burned by refugees to cook meat and the rail line was where they slept. How "beat"—is that not the word? All those expats who had not fled in time—though where would they have gone?—could not drive, since the gasoline had already run out. And they couldn't stay put, for the human wave was rising, and fire came behind it. So they joined their new brothers and sisters and began the painful long climb to Mexico City, the high plateau at the heart of our land.

So many had come to us already, we were bedeviled by our own popularity. We are generous people, and we did our best. I believe we would have managed the crisis if not for the cataclysms to come. But none among us could see the future.

You might recall the greatness of our city, the magnetic draw of our nights. We were the New World City, bigger than New York. More beautiful, more dangerous, more stylish. We were near twenty-five million in the valley, and daily more came. What other city was also the nation itself? There is no Argentina City. No Nigeria City. No USA City. Ce Anahuac, One World—One Mexico.

Outsiders' cars were banned. The moneyed Africans came to my neighborhood of Iztapalapa. Cubans and Chinese took penthouses in the center of the city. Undocumented gringos sucked up real estate and apartments and great homes in Lomas de Chapultepec. In the 2020s, we had managed to clear the air by cutting coal emissions, limiting auto exhaust, and launching the famous government program that set out to plant some million trees in the city and on the outskirts and on the slopes of El Popo, the great father-volcano. It looked like the American state of Colorado up there when the pines and aspens grew, though a haze of yellow smog still wafted across those slopes. Trees and solar and wind. We were mending, we believed. But what we lacked was water. The theory held that trees would inhale carbon and clear the air and cool our skies, and they would exhale water vapor to bring us rain. But the walkers kept coming. And the parks filled with bodies. And the old empty buildings were filled. And the barrios and alleys. With their fires and their smoke and their shit and their bodies. We had nowhere to go.

Still, we were not beaten. Over and again, we have claimed our patrimony as the center of the world, the greatest civilization, the most resilient and creative people.

MCS58

19°25'50.8"N

Only the northern country failed to see it. And we rose, as best we could, to every challenge. For example, this: along with heat, and the droughts that assailed us, there came rageful downpours. Drenching tropical assaults from the hot-seeming clouds. We suffered these, but we are ironists. We appreciated the wicked wit of the earth, drowning us in a time of thirst. Every Mexican child knows that Great Tenochtitlan, the capital of the Aztec world, was built upon a lake. The waters vanished and the buildings appeared and the earthquakes we survived were vicious because the lake bed was clay and mud and the city shook itself apart when the earth moved. And then the water was all sucked from the ground, and the clay beneath our feet hardened and crumbled and the city began its slow entombment as the edifices sank, and the tallest buildings wanted nothing so much as to tip sideways and lie down in exhaustion.

These aguaceros, as we called the drenching rains, were fodder for our computer analyses, and by 2035 the government and the scientists of UNAM assaulted our thirst with Proyecto Tlaloc, perhaps the largest drought amelioration project in history. I was there to see it–I was Tlaloc's contracted historian. Rain seemed at first a further punishing apocalypse–yes it flooded us, yes it brought down mudslides and avalanches, yes the refugees and the poor suffered the most, though we all suffered. But we soon saw it was a reprieve if we had the will to take creative action. The kilometers of standing buildings were perfect water-collecting sites. Like the solar-panel and wind-turbine platforms they had become, we repurposed them. We created vast networks of flumes and reservoirs to slake our valley's thirst. The army, the Red Cross, and hordes of volunteers–many of them, it pains me to say, gringos–evolved instantly into a disorganized but miraculous bureaucracy of hope. Of course, we named this epic movement of assets (you can't imagine the vast array of engineers and laborers and technicians and vehicles) Tlaloc, after the ancient god of rain. The irony of drowning in a universal drought was the subject of many editorials and cartoons when the newspapers still appeared in our city. In 1805, we published the first daily newspaper in Nueva España, and in 2040, ours were among the last.

By any measure, you can see how heroic was our battle.

I am not a superstitious man. If you are reading this, you must understand. In light of what I am about to relate, I must assure you I am a man of letters, a man of reason, a man who rarely even enters a church. But this was Mexico. There came a day when I wondered if Tlaloc the god had actually heard us. I believed he was not impressed. (Indigenous people who still followed the Nahuatl way told us these entities were not gods, but embodiments of the energies of nature, embodiments of elements of our own souls. Westerners did not understand and called them gods. I am a Westerner.)

Tlaloc, too, is an ironist. For the dried lakebed of Texcoco was also a rainfall reclamation area. And the lake, in mockery of our heat plague and of our thirst, began to refill. But the water in the lake was so full now of sewage and chemicals that none could drink it.

I had come to Mexico City from the lush breadbasket of Sinaloa. It was, of course, infamous for drugs and cartels when I was a boy. But the decriminalization of drugs in 2025 gutted their businesses and sent sicarios looking for work as soldiers of fortune and crime enforcers. The days of billions of dollars of illicit profits were over. The crops began to fail anyway, even the lucrative marijuana plantations that rivaled bananas and coffee as Central America's greatest export. Bananas went extinct in the wild, and coffee was losing ground as well. Even the great tobacco corporations of El Norte couldn't rescue the vast marijuana fields, although their research into reclaimed sewage for irrigation saved some communities in the greenbelt states. Water, even stale and badly used water, was the drug of choice by then.

We often looked to the sleeping lovers, Popo and Ixta. Our mountain guardians. Our sentinels. The only place of snows, now bare. Our volcanoes.

I remember saying to my lover, "What is next? Locusts? Rains of blood? Or the volcanoes erupting."

I actually laughed. She put her hand over my mouth.

When the volcanoes erupted, the Little Brother arose and brought with him the old religion of the Night Drinker. Hermanito Jorge. Oh, he was here before. He had many followers on social media. He had all those things that seem absurd now, that seem like legends of a distant past, things our children will doubt in school, will sleep through and get wrong on exams. I have much to say about him, but we must wait just a moment before we become exegetes of the religion of the Hermanito.

When it became clear that the eruptions would not finish us off, that we would continue, as we had continued through every cataclysmic event that ever tried to destroy the heart of Mexico, Jorge told me, "I am the eruption, Joaquin. I am the horseman."

I thought he was part of the history of my country. I thought I'd write books about this era. And this self-made shaman, he thought he was the entire history.

"You are a demagogue," I replied.

We had developed that relationship that Mexican men so enjoy with each other. An intimacy of bluster. A romance of insults.

"You will see, cabrón," he replied.

Anyone who speaks Mexican Spanish will know that *vas a ver* is also a threat. You'll get your comeuppance soon enough.

But I get ahead of myself. The fevers confuse me. To the volcanoes.

What did that old racist Lovecraft call it? "Eldritch horror," I believe. Before I relate the rest of this narrative, our own visit to the mountains of madness, I feel compelled to insist upon my theory as it relates to catastrophe. The human mind, in distress, cannot hold onto reason. And the degradation of the planet is not simply a scientific or ecological conflagration, but also an eroding of the human mind. Reason itself catches fire and burns. The fevers make men see the dead, hear voices, make them think they can fly beside lovers unseen for twenty years. Even the hills and lakes went mad. The earth itself had typhoid. The hallucination of history broke loose among us.

Popocatepetl (Mountain That Smokes) has always been our sentinel, the volcano both loved and feared throughout time. The place where Mexicans could look to see snow–that most unlikely Mexican vista. Father of pines and deer. Maker of clouds. Even the epicenter of the UFO crazes in Mexico City during the 1990s and early 2000s. The very volcano Malcolm Lowry wrote about in *Under the Volcano*. And Popo was stern with us. He erupted in sequences that inspired Chilangos to mount Popo-cams that celebrated its paroxysms on such old platforms as Twitter. They called themselves Twiteadores.

Like the creeping heat and the rising seas, its eruptions became regular to us. We shrugged one shoulder in old-school Mexican fashion and drank toasts to him in our bars. Never believing the worst could happen, for this was mere gringo paranoia, or the fretfulness of the rich and the bourgeoisie. Disruption was not what they wanted, and they were moving to Aspen and Nueva York—one of which flooded and began to rot as soon as they got there. This amused us.

When Popo erupted, truly erupted, it was an explosion that shattered the top third of the mountain and bombarded the city with missiles of burning rock. His being seventy kilometers from Mexico City was a true blessing. We believed the lava and gases would never reach us.

Then his bride, the great Iztaccihuatl (The White Woman) chose to die with her lover and erupted shortly thereafter. Scientists spoke of crustal torsion, an agony of the earth's surface wrenched by forces like the weight of the water, triggering fault lines. But the Mexicans knew better. Izta's suicide was the stuff of ranchera ballads.

She scolded us like a mother gone mad. The earth heaved as the pyroclastic flows of boiling ash asphyxiated and burned whole communities, and lava raised tsunamis of fire, and the ground beneath our feet became waves that toppled even the cathedral of the Virgen de Guadalupe. Our towers fell. The national cathedral on the Zocalo, built by the Aztec slaves of Cortez's Inquisition forces, constructed of the shattered stones of the Temple of the Sun and the great temples of the old city, came apart and spilled across the wrenching earth. The figurines of old gods freed at last from between the Catholic stones, placed there by devout pagans who could pray to their sleeping lords rather than the invader Christ. Looters dared the toppling walls to crush them while stealing the gold still in the rubble.

Hermanito organized armies of heroes through his network: social media, if one could raise a signal. Shortwave radio for others. Runners in the old Aztec style as well, making their ways across the crumbling earth. His followers dug through the ruin with their bare hands and rescued the famous image of the Virgen, thrown to the floor but—of course, it was a miracle!—undamaged. They carried it to the top of Tepeyac, the lovely little hill where she had once appeared to the Indian Juan. There, they guarded her day and night.

If I may offer you one thought about Mexico, it is this: the past is not in the past. Even if the pagan spirits do not exist, we summon them into being. And this we did.

No reasonable people took the Little Brother seriously before the eruptions. Hermanito Jorge, his nom de guerre, was borrowed from both the native healer communities and the evangelical missionaries. The Little Brother rose from the millennial UFO cults that flourished on Mexican social media. The Christ-was-an-astronaut crowd. He also served as an astrologer on one of the Telemundo afternoon talk shows, where he donned golden robes and frolicked with dyed-blonde actresses and dapper Eurotrash-fashioned male hosts. He quickly traded on his minor fame to host a series of very popular vlogs about the narco world that was still flourishing in that era. Interestingly, the narcos themselves seemed to appreciate his reporting. He was not harmed, at any rate. And he was clearly becoming wealthy–there was a vibe (is that the word? una vibra?) about him reminiscent of the old televangelists. For Hermanito Jorge had a specific theme: that narcos and sicarios, without knowing it, had begun reenacting Aztec human sacrifice rituals. Their worsening depredations, lovingly chronicled on video, fed the gruesome interests of working-class Mexico. The people who read the weekly tabloid *Alarma!*, with its infamous photographs of murder, torture, dismemberment, accidents, suicides, read it right till the end. *Alarma!* never went out of print.

Hermanito Jorge maintained that the reenactment of sacrifice would awaken the old gods, who would come to the portals between worlds, thinking that we had returned to their true religion. But that sooner or later, their joy would collapse into rage. These sacrifices were not loving gestures, were not ceremonies beseeching them for mercy and increase, but irreligious acts of greed and commerce. He had to keep the most heinous images off of broadcast television.

But Hermanito was a sensation on his vlog, avidly and breathlessly reporting on the horror. Yes. Conrad: "The horror. The horror." He posted everything he found. A pornography of death and suffering. So much so that the torturers sent him clips seemingly shot for his use. He was decried and denounced, but his followers were legion. And their numbers grew. Amidst this abattoir, he also floated more sedate paranoias: he chased conspiracies and "proved" over and over the imminent return of Planet X, the fabled Nibiru. For decades, this cosmic invader had been mere miles behind our sun, Hermanito warned, about to appear and disgorge alien overlords, The Nephilim, the Watched Angels who would impregnate Earth women. He was so obsessed with invasion that we intellectuals named him Hermanito Trump. What did he care? He had three million followers, and his podcast had an international audience–they said he was especially popular in Colombia, a land with its own burden of magical thinking and upheaval.

Twitter, by then, had already collapsed and been abandoned, and Hermanito Jorge was quick to plant his flag upon the new "Latinx" messaging community, known as Chayo. The Chayonauts were especially active in Mexico City. We elders didn't understand their newspeak. Mexico City, for example, had gone on Chayo from being known as CDMX to merely X. If you were connected to the apocalypse culture, the evolution was clear. If you hadn't followed, you really didn't understand what Hermanito Jorge meant when he launched the meme: XT.

XT HAS RETURNED.

XT REAPS HIS HARVEST.

XT FOR THE NEW SKIN.

XT IS THE SACRED NIGHT DRINKER.

Hermanito Jorge found me for a monstrous reason.

I state this now: he was not a monster. In spite of the horror he brought, in spite of the gruesome death, he was without horns or a tail. In the beginning, his followers fed the refugees. They led the weary to shelter. They used their communication devices (plastic walkie-talkies from La Target) to send civilian guards to protect the Museum of Anthropology–armed men stood watch before the great Aztec calendar that had not even cracked in the tumults. The Little Brother himself had made a camp on one of the ancient chinampas in Xochimilco. He ruled from there. Those old floating islands made by the native people of the lake, still vibrant, still afloat, still rich with chiles and frijoles and what corn was left. The Little Brother's doctrine was proven by these spring-fed watercourses: the past is alive, forever. The spirit of the old ones will forever flow.

Jorge Makasehua (the invented Mexican name Hermanito fancied) was a small man, quick to laugh. Generous and loving with children and the poor. Like me, he was a kind of historian. As the climate shifted, so did the podcasts and the Chayo feed. In the growing vacuum of political leadership, people were seeking guidance. Hermanito Jorge offered solutions that fed their emotions.

I risk the reader's impatience by stepping back, just for a moment. When I first began my studies and writings in Mexico City, it was the end of the 1990s. It seems Edenic now. I had arrived from Culiacan with my history degree and my training in writing historical books from my grandfather.

My area of expertise was the roots of our culture, specifically the ancient gods. I state here, although my countrymen will take offense: the Mexican gods were terrifying. For example, Tlaloc, our beloved rain god, was satiated only by the tears of the innocent. So before they were sacrificed, children were tortured until they cried. And their tears were collected. And then they were publicly sacrificed. Perhaps the reader will forgive me this immodesty, but I had a reputation as a popularizer of history and myth. I could tell the stories. Which is why Jorge came to me, to talk about Ehecatl, the god of wind.

I confess to a fondness for Ehecatl. I don't know why–being the god of the winds somehow made him seem like a rock star. I suppose wind equaled song in my mind. I imagined him as some Jim Morrison figure. You might meet him at a crossroads north of the city, in the shadows of the great pyramid of Teotihuacan. In my mind, Ehecatl wore a zoot suit and had a raven feather in his brim.

You may recall the discovery in 1999 of "Aztec death whistles." I happen to have been with the anthropologists when they uncovered sacrificial victims clutching these carved stone skulls in their skeletal hands. The size of an infant's skull, these carvings had hideously open mouths and looks of utter anguish on their semi-fleshed faces. These were in the hands of people sacrificed to Ehecatl. My old rock god. I chronicled the find in a series of articles. But none of us was prepared for the one researcher with enough imagination to wonder, much later, why these skulls had holes in the tops of their heads, and open mouths. He blew through a skull one day, and we broke and ran when we heard what emanated: the skull shrieked with the voice of a human being slowly slaughtered. Utter terror overtook us. This was the sound of sacrificial Tenochtitlan.

Even at the very end, one could buy replicas on websites, and the replicas screamed like dying women under the knife.

I was presented with one of these ghastly skulls in thanks for my chronicle of the find. Feeling a shudder of irrational fear upon taking this accursed artifact home, I locked it inside a cabinet where it would be safe and out of sight.

But somehow Hermanito Jorge knew I had the whistle. And he wanted it.

He startled me over our first dinner, off the Zocalo in that wonderful café where the waiters floated Malbec wine atop a small sea of pinot grigio, and the roasted corn exploded in the mouth. Gone now. But the gods were capricious, and in the middle of devastation one would find entire blocks unscathed. And so this café, which for a time survived without even one window cracked, one day vanished when the flooded underground metro opened a sinkhole.

After enjoying a robust jousting session of me mocking his beliefs and him jovially dismissing my "false scientific/historical reason," we sat back and basked in the glow of a fine cognac and a dessert of small camote empanadas. We, among the last western degenerates of the gone world before the lava made its way from the outskirts, wise people heading north, all the pilgrims climbing into the ruins thinking they might escape. We were connoisseurs of the end of days.

"It's all illusion," Jorge said.

"It is what we have."

"We have nothing. The president has fled," he said. "The army has fled. Neighborhoods are small empires now. It is like the 1500s. Before Cortez. Do you see? We are tribes again."

"Help will come," I said.

He laughed.

"Help? Who will help?"

I thought about it.

"I have no fucking idea."

He laughed again.

"I need your screaming skull," he said abruptly.

MCS58

19°25'50.8"N

"Hell no."

"You hate it. It frightens you."

"Indeed."

"Do you know why?"

"If you heard it, you'd know why."

"It is summoning the spirits. You don't want to be there when they arrive."

"No mames, guey," I said. I took a drink. "The whistles were to frighten enemies in battle."

"Oh really. Is that your theory?" He nodded and shrugged. "This is why it was clutched in a sacrifice's hand?" He leaned into me. "That is his voice in the skull. His voice. His soul is captured inside the skull. And what you can't hear in the subsonic note, only the spirits hear. They are answering your dead friend's call."

"He's not my friend," I muttered, suddenly not at all amused.

He gestured out the window. Shuffling people like hunched wraiths could be seen against the wavering red light in the sky. How had we found a way to live amidst this chaos? Intermittently, the windows rattled.

"They love you," he said. "They are coming for you. You cannot escape, amigo."

I took him home with me and unlocked my cabinet and thrust the skull into his hands and saw him out. I locked the doors and pulled out an old bottle of Yaqui Bacanora and drank until I could sleep. My dreams were of screaming.

"What Mexico City needs now is a cacique," he said to me at our next and last dinner meeting. "And a high priest."

"And which are you, cabrón?" I asked.

He laughed. He was unnervingly charming. He'd had a craftsman fashion a small gold replica of the screaming skull, which he wore on a black choker around his neck.

"Oh, I am not a politician," he said. "I was hoping, once XT returns, you might be a leader. Joaquin the Cacique."

"And you–"

"The high priest."

I raised a toast to his egomania.

"Do you regret inviting me into your house the other night? If you do, well, so be it."

"I think I do, yes."

He smiled warmly.

"I am the capital now. I am Mexico. My flowers will do my bidding. I can ensure your safety if you but ask."

"Your flowers?"

"Yes. My harvest of millions."

Harvest. Good God. He had gone mad, I thought.

"Well," he said. "You invited me by your own free will." He whispered: "Be careful what you summon."

"I'm leaving."

Lighting a black French cigarette, he said, "Wait. Dear Joaquin, you misunderstand the fate of the world."

"How so? We face extinction."

"Claro, amigo." He leaned forward, breathing smoke into my face. "What you don't understand is that extinction is love."

"Bullshit."

"The gods are hungry."

"Angry?"

"That, too," he said. "But hungry."

"What gods?"

"The true gods."

"And what are they hungry for?"

"They desire revenge. They are hungry for hearts. Flesh. Blood."

"Jesus Christ," I responded.

He smiled almost shyly.

"Not exactly."

Honestly, Hermanito Jorge slipped easily from my mind. I was never interested in the cultish activities or superstitious manias that were springing up everywhere in this world, struggling to understand the apocalypse. Jorge's obsessions seemed to echo every other millennial upheaval through the ages. But this time, they were almost fifty years too late. The millennium had come and gone. I was more interested in hard fact, science and history.

Then, one day in Garibaldi, I saw it. A billboard with the letters XT and the visage of an Aztec god. I knew with the rationality of a bad dream that Jorge truly believed he could resurrect the ancient and terrible gods. I knew to the depth of my soul that he believed the ferocity of the old religions was a form of ghastly future grace. I backed away from the billboard. I knew that for Jorge, our only hope would be in the gift of blood.

It suddenly made chilling sense to me: XT was not a place or a thing, but a being. An old god. The one god of all our mythologies that terrified me. Xipe Totec. If you who find this chronicle do not know how to say such a name, try saying this: *Sheep eh Toltec*. Leave out the *L*. But I beseech you, do not say it out loud.

The God of the Harvest. Also known as the Flayed One. The Skinned God. Father of Suffering. And the Night Drinker. I took that last to be his most poetic name, for does not the harvest drink the night rain? Xipe, who brought our food from the ground. Xipe, who cared for the corn, the sacred grain of the New World, the holy food debased into corn chips and whiskey and syrups that added fresh poison to manmade drinks engineered to taste like the fruits and berries Xipe brought us in bright fields and shady valleys. Xipe, who knew that the bounty of the earth, the easy inspiration of poets and lovers, seemed gentle but was not. The birth of the plant from the seed was violent and torturous. The earth had to break to allow life free rein. And the exhausted earth required the corpses not only of expired plants, but of the rotting creatures who walked upon the plants, who fed on them and on each other. The earth and the flowers were eaters of the dead. Drinkers of their blood. Death, then life; agony, then relief; resurrection, then harvest.

My fear was visceral. Statues of the god always show a grimacing deity seemingly in pain. And hanging from his wrists, extra hands. From his ankles, extra feet. Flat empty breasts flap upon his chest. Over his penis, drooping reproductive organs. For Xipe Totec has been flayed. He lives without skin, his nerves bared and raw.

Like the seeds, he needs to be covered. And our flesh is his personal soil. He loves you as he peels away your soil with his obsidian knife.

As a boy, I read that his priests flayed human sacrifices alive, and wore their pestilential skins until they rotted away and new ones were collected.

I had nightmares of these priests dancing in the plaza with their lips singing from between the lips of the dead.

And then one night, my satellite phone buzzed. All cell lines were down after the eruptions. Landlines were long forgotten.

"We are coming to your house," Hermanito Jorge said.

"Who is?"

"We priests."

"Why?"

"You are the historian. You must witness."

"Witness what, cabrón!"

"The ceremony. It is time. The Lord has come."

"Time for what?" I yelled.

"The first sacrifice. You are my witness."

"Go to hell!"

"Hell is outside your door."

They kicked it open and rushed in.

They were in loincloths and feathers. They were painted in grotesque caricature of what they imagined Aztec warriors might have looked like. They had bound my arms to my sides and my ankles tight to each other. "Am I to be a sacrifice?" I cried. They ignored me. "Please. Please, Jorge." He gently patted my head as they carried me.

The sky was bright red as the mountains continued to melt. These priests were burned all over their bodies, for cinders and sparks fell around us. Some of them had ribbons of blistered skin blowing behind them as if they themselves had been flayed. I passed out when they threw me into the back of a flatbed truck.

I awoke to the screams and moans. The smell came to me as I opened my eyes in the dark. Why be coy? I smelled blood. Enough blood that the air was moist, humid.

I was bound upright to a pole, and the red glow far behind us lit the strange scene. I could tell from the position of the light, and the silence aside from the cries, that we had gone north. Into farming territory. In the distance, I saw houses burning.

As my eyes adjusted, I saw Jorge's minions walking under a vast framework, a kind of long trellis, and thrusting spears up through its roof which I realized was made of human beings. They were tied, men, women, and children, facedown across the wooden slats. The spear carriers stabbed those sacrifices until they stopped writhing and crying out. But their blood pattered like a small rainstorm.

Jorge appeared beside me.

"Behold," he said. "The Night Drinker ceremony."

"What have you done?" I think I said. In spite of my bindings, I was shivering in fear.

"The Flayed One, amigo." Jorge was smiling. "The rain brings life to the fields, the harvest. Our beautiful little brothers, the seedlings beneath the soil are drinking our love."

"You're fucking crazy."

"And the god," he continued, as if he hadn't heard me, "comes to drink his fill as well."

"There is no god here."

He put his hands on either side of my head and gently turned my face. I squinted. There, in the darkest shadows beneath the human trellis, I saw a figure. There are no words for this creature. I, the man of words, fail utterly before the alienness of this apparition. For there was no etheric dark angel there. It was a human figure, but one taller than any man I'd seen. The feathers he had tied to himself seemed, in that darkness, almost to be tentacles.

"I thought he'd be smaller," I blurted, stupidly.

"Dios!" Hermanito Jorge called out, then fell to his knees and put his face in the dirt.

The figure turned and looked us over. I began to twist against the ropes, harder, more desperately. And he came forward. I watched him walk. The blood on his face and chest caught glimmers from the volcanoes. He moved lightly, like some bloodied deer. Like some god.

He paused before me, tied helplessly to this pyre.

His face was covered by the face of another.

His eyes pondered me through the leathery eyeholes of the sacrifice he wore.

His partially covered lips grinned.

He spoke. His breath was cool. It smelled of honey, and poppies, and sweetgrass, and agave. He knew my language.

"Is it not beautiful, my child?" He looked over his shoulder at the writhing bodies dying above him. "You must see beyond what you see," he said. "You must see the world as it gives birth."

I was openly weeping now.

"You must break for me, as I am flayed for you. Tell my story."

Then his hot, raw palm, sticky and pestilential, rose, cupped my cheek, and held it still as his two sets of lips descended to kiss my own.

NEW JESUS
by Tommy Orange

MY NIECE TINA WAS VISITING us from the mountains for the summer and couldn't understand that we just walk in water now. It's not a big deal, but Tina is young and entitled and one of these new mountain elevation people who don't see eye to eye with us sea-level dwellers, we the coastal flooded. The first day she was here her socks got soaked and she sneezed excessively in the evening to the point that I thought she was trying to make us feel bad.

"You can't make yourself sneeze, Herold," my wife Dolorothie said to me.

"You can if you yank nose hairs out, that makes *me* sneeze," I said.

"She wasn't yanking nose hairs out with tweezers while we weren't looking to make us *feel* bad," Dolorothie said, looking out the kitchen window like there was something wrong out there, but what was wrong was in us, was me.

"You don't need tweezers, you can do it with your fingers, you just have to simulate tweezer-grip by putting your fingernails together and yanking."

"Yanking?"

Dolorothie was right, of course. Tina's feet had just gotten too wet, and the cold in Oakland seeps into your bones, the moisture gets through, she's used to high mountain air, thin against human skin it can't penetrate, so yes, Tina had maybe caught the beginning of a cold, but wasn't she emphasizing the sneezes in an unnatural way? This made me distinctly upset, this not knowing if she was leaning into her sneezes or if she really was getting sick.

I should clarify about how much water we walk in. It's not as if we always walk in water, it's that the tide has risen, comes higher when it comes. There's not always water we have to walk in but it's there more often than it's not. We'd wanted to leave, but couldn't afford to just up and go. We got used to it, got used to the storms and floods and the heat, got used to knowing the end of the world had finally arrived not with a bang but a whimper, or a series of minor disasters. Actually too many people call it the end of the world when the world, the earth, would be just fine without us, better off actually, give or take an era or eon or age or whatever amount of time the world might need to get over us.

We hung Tina's socks out on the drying line in the backyard, and I told her she'd be better off not wearing socks outside during her visit. Tina's my estranged sister Valerie's only daughter.

"I'm so many things I'm not even a thing," Tina told me and Dolorothie regarding her background, her heritage, or her blood, because I'd asked her if we were from the same tribe.

"But are you enrolled in our tribe? It's not about blood, it's about having citizenship in a sovereign nation. That's what it used to mean, anyway."

"Citizenship in a sovereign nation?" Tina said, with a distrustful look in her eyes.

"Your mom didn't explain any of it to you?"

"It's that my dad is Chinese and Thai and Italian and other white things. I can't even remember all of them."

"I'm not even sure the tribe's still together and organized in Oklahoma anymore," I said. Tina wasn't the least bit interested in what I was talking about.

"So what do *you* do when your feet get cold?" she asked my wife, avoiding my eyes.

Most people around here don't wear socks, and not even shoes either but porous rubber clogs. There's a saying from Hammon, Oklahoma, the small town where my dad grew up, and it goes, "It's Hammon, man, no socks." I'm not sure what sense it made for my dad, or for my Cheyenne relatives in Oklahoma, but here in Oakland, in the year 2040, it makes utter sense. We live wet lives but our feet need not stay wet with socks. There are wood-burning stoves to warm our feet by and socks inside—we wear socks in the house, we're not insane people. The future turned out not to be as futuristic as everyone thought. The weather slowed everything down. Anyone who *could* leave left for higher, stormless ground a long time ago. Tina was *born* in the mountains, so this is her first time down to the coast. Everyone's gotten so used to it here we don't even talk about it anymore. The water. People walk their dogs in it, their babies in strollers with aquadynamic design. Jogging is doable most of the time. Sometimes it's so shallow that if the light hits it right it looks like we're walking on water. No one even talks about Jesus anymore. The end of the world came and went too many times and Jesus failed to show, or it was because science proved to be right about climate change, and had always stood diametrically opposed to religion. Or we lost the need or ability to have faith. I don't really know.

Down from the mountains, Tina brought word of a New Jesus. At first I thought it seemed like lazy naming, New Jesus, but then for the books it's just the Old then New Testament so it makes a kind of sense. My dad always used the word *Creator*. This was often the Native stand-in name for Jesus. He would use *Creator*, *God*, or *Jesus* interchangeably. Christianity had been shoved down the throats of Native people since contact but in worse and worse ways; the tighter and more normalized the government's grip became, the more effectively Christianity through colonization exercised its control. That's why I would never be a Christian, had never considered it. Even though my dad believed that when he died he would be in heaven with Jesus. The old one. Indian stuff is complex.

"New Jesus lives in each of us and is our action," Tina said. No one had asked her to elaborate on New Jesus. "New Jesus is our cooperation with each other and with the earth. We all become new in New Jesus when we take care of and love one another. The whole world is New Jesus waiting to be realized."

"Gobbledygook," I said without meaning to say it out loud. Tina didn't back down or get her feelings hurt like I thought she might, she came straight for me.

"I'm sorry, Herold, if we still believe in goodness, and don't want to let the ethical murkiness that got us into this mess flood our lives with ruin." She really said that.

Flood our lives with ruin. I laughed and Dolorothie looked at me with something nestled between deep concern and pity.

"Why does it have to be Jesus again?" Dolorothie asked Tina. I liked Dolorothie's line of questioning.

"Yeah, and what makes New Jesus new?" I asked.

"We aren't waiting for him to come back anymore. We've redefined his holy location. It's here. It's like he talked about. The kingdom of God is here. Now."

"All this talk of him, and kingdom, it feels so... outdated. Why give god gender at all?" Dolorothie said.

"That's the beauty of it all, and part of why it's New Jesus—it's matriarchal. And by still using Jesus we've been able to recruit people we wouldn't have been able to recruit before. It's like how Christians adopted pagan rituals to be more appealing. A belief system needs to be big enough for there to be community. We need each other."

"Interesting," Dolorothie said. At that point Tina and I both said, "What is?" in an overeager way. We were both worried about which side of interest she fell on. I didn't want the conversation to continue.

"Remember we have that thing tomorrow, early, Dolorothie, we should get some sleep," I said, and gestured with my head toward the stairs leading up to our bedroom. We really did have a thing. We were helping friends pack up their house; they were moving. I wasn't looking forward to it. They were more Dolorothie's friends than mine, but it worked as an excuse to leave Tina in the kitchen alone with her New Jesus.

We left Tina at home to help our friends move. We found out that day that they were moving onto a boat to try their hand at seafaring. This was something people are doing, living on the water. Fishing for sustenance. It makes a kind of sense. One of the first movies I ever saw in the theater was *Waterworld*, with Kevin Costner. It was right after I saw him save so many Indians in *Dances with Wolves*, at which time he was briefly a hero of mine. Our world is not like *Waterworld*, with pirates and filtering pee for drinking water and white girls with dreads, but more and more people are living on boats and dependent on sustenance from fishing. This also means fish is one of our main sources of protein, is more often than not the only meat to eat.

Dolorothie felt bad leaving Tina to herself all day so we took her out to dinner when we got home. Mainly it was fruit and seafood, a combination we've come to master, which it seems strange now was never a thing before, it pairs so well. Raspberries and salmon, tuna and mango, strawberry trout, it just works. Tina didn't *trust* the fish so she only ate the fruit. Blackberries. When we went for a walk after dinner, Tina continued to complain about the water, this time about the murkiness, how she didn't like not being able to see what she was stepping in.

"Too much water breeds bad life," Tina said to us.

"What kind of bad life do you mean?" I said.

"This bad life," she said, pointing all around us.

"Now that's going a little too far, from someone who... We've invited you into our home, now you take that back, Tina," I said. When she didn't I called her a hillbilly. Dolorothie really didn't like that I said that, felt that I'd stooped to outdated insults. I went upstairs, afraid I'd say something worse, afraid I was undoing our life by opening my mouth, by letting Tina get to me, by letting my insecurities get to me about what Dolorothie might really think about the way we lived, whether she thought of it as good or bad.

After sulking in the bedroom, trying but failing to read, to focus enough to comprehend anything from the several novels I keep on my desk, waiting for Dolorothie to possibly come tend to me, I went downstairs and heard Tina and Dolorothie talking.

"It's really all about finding a way to love everything," Tina was saying.

"I don't know if that's healthy," Dolorothie said.

"You have to rethink your thought patterns, you have to redo thinking altogether, you have to become New," Tina said.

"What does becoming new do for you?" Dolorothie said.

"Everything, just everything, Auntie," Tina said. I'd had enough.

"D'you care for some coffee or tea, dear?" I said to Dolorothie, strolling into the living room. Tina seemed startled, then recovered.

"I'd love some," Tina said to Dolorothie.

"No, thank you," Dolorothie said to me.

"Which one?" I asked Dolorothie about what Tina wanted.

"Tea," Tina said to Dolorothie. I went and made her tea. Their conversation about New Jesus did not continue that night, but over the following weeks, if I left the house, whenever I came back the two of them would go quiet around me like they didn't want me to know they had been talking. Could this have been paranoia? The thing about paranoia is that as soon as you start getting paranoid about para-noia you're lost. You have to follow through with conviction. But Dolorothie had become quieter about Tina. Less vocal about Tina's presence, with her ideas about life in the mountains.

"You're not really buying into this New Jesus business, are you?" I asked Dolo-rothie in our bedroom before bed one night.

"Buying in... business... interesting," Dolorothie said, keeping her head down in a book.

"What does *that* mean?" I said. "What book is that?"

"None of your *business,*" she said.

"Tina's leaving in a few days, I was thinking we should have some friends over and give her a farewell party."

"You sound ridiculous," Dolorothie said. Something was wrong. Further along than I thought. Dolorothie had always been a little sad, a little susceptible to beliefs requiring faith, but these had been related to her garden, or to aesthetic theories regarding interior design, never religion, and never like this.

Lying there next to my wife that night I got it into my head to tie Tina up in our flooded basement, to convince her she was wrong about how much better life was in the mountains, and to tell Dolorothie she had changed her mind and come around to see things the way we see them. I would get her down there by convincing her to come see the family of albino smooth newts that had showed up one day to stay, probably because it's so cool and moist down there. I would use the albino smooth newts, claiming they were poisonous to make her promise she'd have one of her talks with my wife, only this time to convince her that *we* had the good life and that mountain life was the bad life and that she was leaving immediately to go get her stuff and move down here and renounce New Jesus.

"You're going to have to do something about the roof," Dolorothie said to me before turning out the light to go to sleep. There was an audible drip in the corner of the room. That *I* was going to have to do something about the roof concerned me. We normally used the royal we concerning the house, anything related to the life we lived together.

"There's a new sealant I heard about that's supposed to be pretty long-lasting," I said. But she was already asleep.

The next day I slept in until noon. I never sleep in, much less that late. I suspected them of drugging me right away. But how? Had I stayed up all night worried in bed? Yes, but I must have gotten some sleep at some point. That I didn't know should have worried me more.

I checked the closet and found Dolorothie's clothes mostly gone. I borrowed a neighbor's car and headed out for Copperopolis, the town where Tina lives. It was two hours away. We'd only been there once years ago for my sister's wedding. I remember Dolorothie saying more than once that she loved it up there. I hadn't thought of it again until then. We were maybe not the happiest couple, not the happiest people, but we had our life together and it was not a bad one. I'd never imagined her wanting to leave. My neighbor's car had no radio so I was stuck with my own head and the sound of the wind moving through the car, the low rumble of the road. I searched my memory for clues about Dolorothie's unhappiness. I knew she didn't like the storms and the floods and that she was palpably happier when the sun was out. Had I ever asked if she wanted to move? Never mind that we couldn't afford it. Though maybe that's why I'd never asked, why the subject had never been broached until Tina came down and made it all possible. Tina's mom had a nice piece of land up there. Just a trailer on the land but land nonetheless, with oak trees and wild horses, chickens in a coop and wandering deer. Turkeys. But Jesus. New Jesus. She would have invited us up when the shit started hitting the proverbial fan years ago but for that she knew I wasn't and would never be a believer. As much as it was supposed to be new and about love, it was still a sin to live with worldly people, even if they were family. End-of-the-worldly people like Dolorothie and me would never have been accepted up there.

*   *   *

I was maybe halfway there when it started raining. Hard. Out of nowhere. I swore the sky'd been cloudless, blue. Maybe not. Either way it came down so hard I had to pull over. Where I pulled over was not ideal, as it was next to a ditch and kind of sunken in even where I'd parked. The rain was so loud and relentless. It was coming down in sheets. Gallons of rain pounding the car. It's not like I hadn't been in a heavy rain before. It was how loud it was against the roof of the car, it was being so alone and desperate, it was feeling like someone or something from above was telling me something. Did I think it was New Jesus? Not at all. But after half an hour of relentless rain, I was afraid. What if it didn't stop? What if there was nothing but rain now? There were places that got weird weather like that and ended up underwater, non-coastal towns. I felt bad for being in a car. I'd sworn them off after everything that happened had seemed so based on cars. Cars and cows and planes and men. The rain kept coming at the same rate and volume. Dumping. And I'd been dumped. That's what had happened. Taking your clothes and leaving and not saying anything was dumping someone. Did I think I would save her? She was being saved by New Jesus. I told myself that if the rain would just let up, I'd do the same, I'd turn around and go home, let Dolorothie do what she wanted, come home or not. Dolorothie didn't need me saving her any more than Indians ever needed Kevin Costner types to save them. I could let go of the fact that I wouldn't get closure if she didn't come back, that we wouldn't have our last words together. If this was about god, about New Jesus, who was I to interfere? But the rain didn't stop. At one point I got out of the car and fell to the ground from the water pressure. That's what it felt like, like weight pushing me down. I couldn't see five feet in front of me in any direction. The rain was roaring. I got back in the car and thought about who I would pray to if I were to pray. Help from where? I closed my eyes and leaned my head against the steering wheel. I remembered my first time seeing the ocean. My dad brought me to Half Moon Bay and told me that the first time he'd seen the ocean he was already a father. I couldn't believe how big it was, how vast, and how it came at the land with such force, such power, the waves. I asked my dad what made it do that. He told me Creator.

As the rain continued to pour down I felt a kind of softening in my heart for Tina, who had been raised up Christian, too, and was so many things she wasn't even a thing. She was Indian, too, even if she was so many things besides, even if she wasn't enrolled. She didn't know better. I couldn't blame Tina. Dolorothie was bigger than that.

I'm not sure how much time passed. It seemed like the rain couldn't possibly keep up its intensity for much longer, which made time seem to pass impossibly slow, or not pass at all. At one point I opened the car door again and saw that the water was almost a foot up, that the rain had collected in this sunken area along the highway along the Altamont Pass where there used to be windmills as far as the eye could see. When I closed the door I thought I felt the car slip a little. Was it sinking? I thought of the ocean again, and of my dad, and his belief. Then I did something I'd never done before. I wouldn't call it praying, but that's probably what it was. With all the windows rolled up, I said, almost as if to the car, I said, *Thank you for what I've had, how I've managed with what I haven't been allowed, and thank you for getting me this far. I'm sorry I haven't done more.* It felt good. Like I'd done something good for someone I loved. Not for myself. Some bigger body I'm a part of. I half expected to be thanked, for the rain to let up a little, or altogether, but it didn't. I don't know what it was about the fact that the water was rising and I didn't care that it was. I'd never felt such a sense of dread and possible freedom at the same time before. I laughed a laugh that turned into a cry that made me so sad I wanted to fall asleep. Something had been wrong for a long time. And it was me.

THE
GOOD PLAN
by Mikael Awake

THE CRISIS WAS COMING OR it was here or it had just passed, I forget. What I remember is everyone wanted to go home, which for me was no longer a where, but a who: my mother, who was dying.

I remember checking the departure time over the boarding door, then looking out through the window at the plane, empty on a rainswept runway, a family of birds asleep on the wing.

Though there was no telling when, or if, we would leave, the Good People were patient. No one stood or paced, no one transferred weight from one foot to the other, no growls of frustration. Even if the faces of those around me hadn't been hidden behind surgical masks, I still wouldn't be able to recall them now. Whether they were scared or bored or were a different color or if color mattered or what. The Crisis had brought so many loud, bad things, who could remember how these other quiet, good things had arrived, like this patience at a boarding gate? It was best for everyone to believe that things had always been this way.

The only Good People who were lacking patience were my escorts, who lived within the walls of the hub and wanted to return to their families before the river took the highway. The escort on my left took a breath through his surgical mask and shifted in his seat. "Crisis a-coming," he said.

The one on my right never looked up from weather alerts on his phone. "Heard that one before."

The Crisis erased faces, names, borders, including the one between Before and After, which was already blanching. The Crisis came not once, but again, and once again, bearing other names depending where it hit, though "Crisis" is the only one I can recall.

The Good People needed to remember how it had been before the Crisis, so they began to pay us to forfeit memories for cash. By forgetting, I could survive.

Over us, a TV played footage of droughted fields far away and coastal hubs that would have been destroyed by water but for the walls the Good Plan had built around them. This was the only show left. If there were once other shows, I could not remember them. In one shot, I recognized the place I had fled. The name of the country escapes me. Somewhere with an *E*. "Escape" maybe.

I made a dry cluck with my tongue and glanced toward the restroom, and my escorts played rock-paper-scissors to see who would walk me, arguing over the rules of the game, until the argument turned into the game, which someone won by being loudest. The one who lost jerked my arm painfully. "Let's go." The green windbreaker over my shackles fell to the carpeting, and I remembered something.

"Please," I said, startling them, because until then I had been silent. It was the first word I'd been able to utter—my lungs rebelled against me whenever I tried. When the escorts made no move to pick it up, I wheezed louder, "*Please!*" My voice came out strangled. Good People pressed their masks closer to their mouths, afraid they would catch Hadega from an unmasked.

"Relax, okay," said the escort, draping the jacket back over my wrists.

I remember the burning in my chest, and Good People fastening masks over their children's faces as I passed, looking away. That always made me feel rotten. I remember craning my head under the faucet to drink the chemical-tasting water just as a whistling janitor entered and, seeing us, stopped whistling. "I come back later." I remember thinking about the word *later*. What did later mean to me? I did not have later and neither did my mother, who was the only home left.

This had not been my plan. I was supposed to bring her here to the hub. My sister was supposed to be here. When the Crisis came, it took all our plans, replaced them.

This is the part where I would tell you, if I could remember, who I was and what village I was born in and what I look like and why I was being escorted in chains back to the place beginning with the letter *E*. There is a chance I will get everything wrong: the wan color of our droughted farm, the sunken lines of my father's cheeks as we bathed and shrouded his body for burial, the softness of my mother's hand and my sister's as we walked south for days to a country also beginning with *E*, perhaps also named Escape.

This is the part where I would tell you about the men there who knew how to take people like us across the water to become one of the Good People, safe from the Crisis behind the high walls of a hub, how it was the only way anyone could imagine a later, and how I tried to leave my mother and sister in the refugee camp without ceremony or goodbye in the dead of night, and how she trailed me, stubborn girl, through the brush to the waiting lorry, refusing to be left there alone with our mother, howling at my selfishness, and this is the part where, if I had not forgotten everything, I would tell you about our weeks of thirst and hunger, stalked by the glinting eyes of hyenas, before cramming into a boat bound for the land of the Good People, and the hunger of the sea, of the mouths of black waves that sent us tumbling through the dark endless waters, about our gurgling prayers, about the shrieks from those drowning all around us and from my own mouth as I clawed water and air toward the sound of my sister gasping my name, a name I can't remember, how I grabbed hold of her with a hunger that was greater than any I had ever felt on land and said, "I will never let you go." This is the part where pain would turn me real, if only I could remember.

At first, the Crisis had come with no name, taking our father and his fields and the livestock and the ancestors' promises, making each new day seem longer than the one before. We thought that would change when my sister and I became Good People, but they said Hadega trailed us wherever we went and punished those who rescued us at sea, locking them away in different camps than us. The Good People said we had caused the Crisis. We said the Crisis had caused us. *Hadega* was not their word for us, just the closest one I remember. Soon they even forgot that name and just called us the Crisis. They said that we had brought it with us. We could not work, we could not leave our government housing, they said, for our own protection and the protection of the Good People.

All I wanted was for the days to be the same, but I had no control over them. I felt there was nothing I could control, not even my memories, which came without warning like social workers. The eyes of the drowning people were the eyes of our mother, weeping over video calls saying we had left her to die, and eyes followed me across the borders of sleep. Then the Good Plan came, replacing all that came before it with a dream of life in the walled hubs. Those who refused were sent to the Rear Tier, where they were never heard from again. We gave our memories, and they gave us money. I didn't mind it like the others. It made the days easier when you could erase the feeling of being Hadega. Days became the same, one bled into the next, then into nothingness, and I started to forget everything.

I would be gone from my sister for days at a time, leaving her with food and TV and instructions never to leave our apartment. I no longer had to say, *I will never let you go*. She could see it in my face. Still, she raged and bucked like a mule and shrieked that she needed to find work somewhere, that the air in the walled hubs was making her sick, that she couldn't stand to live with me anymore, pounding the door with her feet and fists as I slid the bolt in place to lock her inside.

For days or months or maybe years, I forfeited memories to the Good Plan to keep us afloat, memories that the Crisis had made worthless. How to plow a field with one ox, how to dig a well, how to mix dirt and water and straw to build a house. Until one night I returned to our building to find its twenty-four stories engulfed in flames, black clouds billowing into a black sky, the useless hoses of the Good People dribbling out rationed water.

And though she herself was nowhere in sight, I collected my sister's green windbreaker from where it lay on the sidewalk, covered with brown-singed freckles from lit embers falling slow as snow. Her name was the smoke filling my lungs as men in gas masks beat us back with batons. It was only right, for I was the Crisis.

Just when I have no breath to say her name, I remember it: Luam. My Luam, trapped in the burning tower of memory.

The escorts and the shackles must have meant I had run out of memories to give. Because I have never done anything wrong in my life. I remember, when I was a boy, kicking a dog once in a while whenever it whined for food. Luam hated when I did that. Maybe that was wrong. I had never even thought to commit a crime, though the pain I felt every time I drew breath felt like punishment.

When they couldn't identify Luam's remains among the burning rubble, they said it was again my fault for not having papers to help the authorities identify her, and my fault for locking her inside, and when I showed them her green windbreaker, they said that that proved nothing. Everything proved to them that I was Hadega, had brought nothing but the reek of Hadega with me from the places beginning with *E* that might have stood for "Enemies" and which, I suddenly realized, was a more fitting place to spend the rest of my days than here, among the Good People.

"We've given you nothing but chances with the Good Plan," said the authorities, and they bristled if we dared question it, for it had always been good to the Good People. The Good Plan had built walls to save cities by the sea, had allowed the Good People to adapt to life after the Crisis. If it hadn't been good, they argued, why had it lured me from where I came? How dare I question it. They refused to hear us. Whatever we said or did made them ever more certain we were Hadega out to destroy the name of the Good Plan and what it had done for the world, and that was really what they could not stand.

The Crisis left no time for debate or nuance, only panic. That's how the Good Plan came to pass, or maybe it was already underway; either way, we were helpless to stop it. All the Good People began to wear masks over their faces and put larger ones made of steel and poured concrete around their towns and countries. The masks shielded from the Crisis. Our faces, on the other hand, remained exposed, unprotected. If Hadega was the Crisis, said the Good People, what was the point of protecting us from ourselves? My chains were part of the Good Plan. This escorted flight back to where I had come from was part of the Good Plan. Maybe I could have stayed longer, forfeiting more memory until I became one of the Good People, or at least forgotten the difference between me and them, mailing money to save her life across the sea that had tried to end mine. The Good People told me I had chosen my chains, but really I had forgotten what chains were.

Good People boarded first: those who were employed by the Good Plan, followed by those who were true believers in it, and finally by those who went along with it because they had no choice. I, an unmasked, a transgressor of the Good Plan, a Hadega, was last to board. Then came an announcement that the Crisis was getting worse, and we were back out at the gate again, waiting patiently for the plane to be cleared for takeoff. My escorts shot me looks like it was my fault they would have to spend the night, or many, on this side of the flooded interstate, waiting out the river's bloat. The family of birds on the wing was no longer there, or maybe they were not there yet, I can't be certain, so I refuse to say.

But we reboarded at some point. I remember being escorted up the aisle once everyone had taken their seats. No eyes met mine, except those of gawking children who had perhaps never seen an exposed face in public before. The escorts finally removed my cuffs before packing me in tight with several other unmasked in the back of the cabin; they thanked me for my participation in the Good Plan. "And sorry if I hurt your arm earlier," said the escort. "You kinda winced."

"Do you forgive me?" he asked, and a bolt of real emotion seemed to flash across what I could see of his face, or maybe it was just allergies.

I don't remember choosing to nod, but I did, and with a bittersweet nod of his own, he locked the gate that separated us from the rest of the passengers.

I remember the backs of the heads of the Good People in rows stretching to the front of the plane. Tilting sideways with sleep. Tilting back to get the last cube of ice from a cup. Headrest screens played footage of the Crisis on a loop. I remember men beside me in the pen using what little memory they had to argue amongst themselves until we landed.

Every so often, someone would say, "The Good Plan *is* the Crisis."

"No, the Good Plan is the only thing that works."

"Does any of it make sense anymore?"

We forgot the things we meant to remember, but whenever we were silent we remembered the things we were trying to forget. We spoke in the same truncated language, using only the words we had needed to survive. *Good. People. Thank you. Please.* There was no need for small talk about the weather. Our memory of other words, of words in our own language and what they meant, could not be trusted. So we went along with the Good Plan, forgetting words like the name of the place beginning with *E*, words like *escape*, thinking it would turn us into Good People. But we were wrong, or we had remembered incorrectly. They told us why we were being sent away in words that we could not understand because we had given ours to them. We had given everything away.

Weary flight attendants paced the aisles serving water and one type of food made from one type of grain. The Good People told themselves they liked not having to make decisions any longer. Efficient. Clear. One drink. One food. When had it been any different? There was only one in-flight TV show to choose from, the same one that had been playing at the gate. Everyone had stopped recognizing it as the same show. Whenever anything changed, many Good People would grow irate, then forget their anger, then forget that things had been any other way, and this had been going on for longer than anyone could remember.

"It's all part of the plan," a flight attendant said, slipping each of us a hardened disk of grain. "Don't worry."

Even though we didn't remember how to worry, our worry remembered us.

Just as my eyelids began to narrow with sleep, we were landing, and when I stepped off the plane, thinking I had made it back to that second place beginning with *E*, I did not recognize it. I could not recall so many buildings falling into disrepair, so many signs in a language that we never used as children. There must have been something wrong. The Crisis must have made the skies unnavigable. When I squinted through the dense haze at what I had assumed was a mountain range surrounding us, I saw that it was, instead, the largest wall I had ever seen.

I waited until it got dark, rubbing the swelling in my arm and wrists, until a man with dirty fingernails and work boots approached me. "You have friends on the Rear Tier," he said, helping me to my feet. We drove in his rusted-out pickup, and he explained how this was not the place that begins with *E*, explained how the Good Plan had taken most of the good cropland there, because nothing would grow anywhere else.

As we exited, we drove past a checkpoint where a long queue of the unmasked stood waiting for approval to enter the hub. "I should join them," I said to the driver. "Let me out." But he only shook his head sadly and kept driving, past industrial zones that slowly gave way to muddy hills and then sleep.

When I woke, the sun was coming up and we were parked outside a gnarled fence made of sideways branches interlaced like fingers. I recognized nothing, but the sight of it tingled something lost in me.

Nor did I recognize my mother as she spoke in hushed tones with the man who had driven me there, and even as she came toward me and wrapped her arms tightly around my body, I could hardly tell it was her. Where was the frail, grief-stricken face from the video calls? Where was the sick person I had sold my memories to save? Who was this glowing woman with silver and black hair? As I staggered from the truck, my eyes found another one standing behind the knotty fence, a younger woman, older and fleshier than I remembered, whose name was slowly emerging from my throat.

"Luam," I said, just as the world went beautifully black, and the ground pulled me to its breast.

And when I revived, after how many hours or days I can't say for sure, I found myself tucked loosely into a narrow bed, lying alone in some darkened room. Through an open window, a breeze blew across my arms, and I could not remember having smelled air so cool or sweet in so long and drank it thirstily into my lungs. When I opened my mouth to speak, my breath tasted clean inside my mouth. I began to call out, but could not finish the word before my body shook with coughs. Footsteps grew louder behind the closed door, and when it opened, there were my sister and my mother with smiles as bright as the lanterns they held near their beautiful faces. Luam, her old green windbreaker snug around her shoulders, reached for my hand, which I drew back. "I have the Hadega," I said, but she sucked her teeth and squeezed my fingers. With every spoonful of my mother's soup lifted to my lips, I remembered another word. My time away had worn my tongue down, the way sea does a stone. Fenugreek. Cardamom. Luam plugged in a radio at my bedside and played back old songs the Good People had paid me to forget.

"Where are we?" I asked. "Is this afterlife?" If we had all died and gone to heaven, I might have understood. I only knew it felt like nowhere I had ever been. They promised they would make me understand when I was ready. The bad memories barged into my dreams each night, even of Luam, who I knew was safe and had made it out of the building that night and found our mother and brought her here and nursed her back to health. As I replaced those bad memories with new ones—the pepper soup, the old songs, their soft hands in mine—sleep came easier, as did speech, as did time.

When I was strong enough to move about on my own feet, I found my mother and Luam outside the front door of our house, kneeling in a garden. In the distance I could see hills shrouded in fog, green tops of trees broken up by white windmills as far as the eye could see. Nowhere could I see the looming walls of a hub. A wooden footbridge arched over a small irrigation stream amid the tomatoes and grains and peas. Butterflies bothered the air. Nearby, a bright red bird fluttered from an immaculate earthen hut with a thatched roof where mason jars of fruit sat pickling on shelves. I did not know where I was or when. Unseen, I leaned in the doorway watching them work in the fading daylight.

"How much of his memory do you think they took?" Luam said to our mother.

Our mother sucked her teeth sadly and continued shoveling rich brown soil into a wheelbarrow abuzz with flies.

"And how long before he sees we aren't home?"

"Home is wherever we are," my mother answered. "And we're here now."

My sister finally looked up and saw me.

"Are you ready to meet the village?" she said.

I braced for the burning in my chest and throat, but felt the words escape my mouth, phlegmy but painless. "What village?"

* * *

This is the part where I would tell you about what happened after the Crisis and the Good Plan, when we began to find more words for what had been happening to us. All I know is we started to remember, not because we were forced to, but because we saw all the damage that forgetting had done.

The next morning, the three of us set off down the path leading away from our cluster of huts, and before long we came to a strip mall. Wisteria had cracked through the sidewalks and the paved parking lot and overtaken a sign for something called The Village Galleria. Luam strolled ahead of us, introducing me to people who stood beside food carts.

"Not what you expected, is it?" said the bread seller, handing me a powdery brown loaf, flaky crumbs tumbling through my fingers. "Welcome to the Rear," she called out, waving as Luam pried open the automatic doors and we entered the mall.

Suddenly, we were standing in a food court, where people sat under trees growing up through the high ceilings overhead. We walked past families with bright plump peppers and bulbs of garlic laid out on waxed blankets in front of them, the ghostly outlines of old restaurant signage behind them. This village, this place, whatever it was, did not seem to belong to us either.

How many still remembered that this was not ours? How many of us had been spared after the Good Plan?

There was more wisteria snaking up and down a broken escalator, and two deer stood watching us cautiously from a raised flower bed across the skylit atrium, and flowering stalks covered the length of what had once been a cosmetics counter. The land was remembering itself. In the middle of the wishing fountain, a fruiting tree shot up from a heap of untouched coins. "Stop," I shouted as Luam reached to pluck a pale yellow fruit from the tree's branches. "You don't know who that belongs to."

I did not know what had happened here, and I did not want to know. It could not have been something good. "It belongs to no one," she said, handing me the small orb, marbled with red, a soft fuzz along its skin, almost like a person's flesh. I cast my eyes around the atrium nervously. I could hear the high-pitched laughter of children somewhere, echoing off the faded cracked marble of this forgotten empire, and even further the muffled sputter of an approaching helicopter.

"Don't be scared," my mother said.

I bit into it and smiled without wanting to.

"What is its name?" I said, wiping sweet dribble from the wiry hairs on my chin. When they said the word in Tigrinya, rolling it around their tongues to make me remember it, I recognized its name, so familiar it could have been my own.

"Do you remember ever tasting anything so sweet?" Luam asked.

Of course, I couldn't. And so we sat there at the edge of the fountain in that perhaps ancient structure, savoring each bite, chewing slowly.

"Who taught this boy how to chew?" said Luam.

The question was not meant for an answer. Like those things most necessary for survival, chewing is kept in the body, despite all we may forget. But mother surprised us both by answering: "Maybe it was hyenas."

And I remember we laughed so hard we couldn't breathe.

HE ARE
THE PEOPLE
by Elif Shafak

"COME OVER HERE," SAID GRANDMA, sitting in the armchair by the window that looked out onto the orchard–that's what we still called it, the orchard, as though by insisting on using its old name we could somehow bring it back to life.

Next to Grandma, in a blue ceramic pot, under the newly watered soil, were the seeds of the herbs she had been trying to grow. Every day she talked to the plants that were there but not yet there. She was good at that, communicating with invisible beings. People who didn't know her well enough might assume it was because she had gone blind with old age that communicating with the unseen came easily to her. But they'd be wrong. She had always been like this, my grandma, even when her eyes were as sharp as an eagle's.

We used to buy our herbs once a week from the local bazaar. A peasant woman with a sallow complexion and withered skin would sell them–herbs in wicker baskets, herbs in colored glass jars that glowed like precious stones. Strings of wild garlic hung around her neck, tangling into her long hair, which was so smooth and shiny and reddish brown it seemed to me as if it were made of hemlock-tanned leather.

Until I met her I never knew that one's hair could be younger than one's face or hands; it had never occurred to me that such a thing might be possible.

The peasant woman would be there every week, rain or shine, sitting under an oak tree, smoking rolled cigarettes, the ground beneath her feet strewn with peeled twigs, decaying leaves, fallen lichens. She spoke with a loud but husky voice, lisping slightly. I listened to her singsong the name of each item on her stall: *Blessed thistle. Lady's slipper. Summer snowflake. False sow thistle...* Sometimes she gave me a smile and a pat on the head; other times, a surprise present: a crocheted doily, a beaded bracelet, and, once, a handkerchief with embroidered borders. Grandma said it was because we were her best customers, but I wanted to believe it meant she liked me. We always want people we like to like us back. Either way, I loved visiting the bazaar, the air filled with mingling smells of fresh fruits and spices, salt and sweat, pickled fish and newly baked bread. But then, little by little, the medicinal herbs started to disappear. The fruits and vegetables too. Then the woman was gone. And one day there was no bazaar to visit anymore, just a few stalls. That was all years ago, but I still saw it in my dreams sometimes–the marbled blocks of halvah, the dried eggplants, the flags fluttering in the wind, the awnings dripping with passing rain...

Since then Grandma had been growing her own herbs in each corner of our garden. Arugula, basil, watercress. But it was not that easy. She was too old to get down on her knees to pull out weeds and snip dead blooms. Besides, there was never enough water. And when there was, there was so much of it that it killed all the native flora. Thus the herbs in the ceramic pot had become Grandma's new obsession. If she could not save them in large numbers, she would save them in smaller quantities.

"Come," she repeated.

Taking a few steps toward her, I waited obediently. Outside the window, I sensed a sudden movement–a faint rustle, brief and vague as a fleeting thought. In the distance the unmistakable drone of an insect, and somewhere nearby a crack, the snap of a parted twig under a careless foot. I held my breath.

No doubt Grandma had heard it, too, but she chose to say nothing. Instead, she leaned forward and murmured my name: "Ada."

She touched my face, first with one hand, then with both. Her skin was rough like crumpled paper–like a letter someone had lovingly written but then, having decided not to send it, balled up and tossed aside. I winced a little when her thumb grazed against my chin. The fingernail on her left thumb had changed so much over the years, becoming thicker and duller, turning a shade of greenish purple reminiscent of cheese gone to mold.

Grandma touched my cheeks, my nose, my lips. She sighed as if she could sense the lies that came out of my mouth sometimes.

"Tell me, did you visit them this morning?"

I nodded. "Yes."

"What did they eat?"

"They had... potato."

"One each?"

"Yeah, one each," I replied, trying to hide the resentment in my voice.

"Two, then... two potatoes." She uttered the last word slowly, as though she could taste it on her tongue. "That's good."

She smiled and sat back, satisfied. I wondered how tall she would be if she didn't have her hunch and could stretch out to the full length of her body.

"Grandma..."

"Hmm?"

"How long are we going to have to keep them here?"

"For as long as needed."

"Yes, but..."

"They have sought refuge in our house, have they not? They are our guests."

I could not help my gaze drifting toward the front door. It was closed. Somewhere behind the door was the stranger. The refugee. She was taking a walk, *out for some fresh air*, putting us all in danger. The toddler was sleeping downstairs in the basement. That's where they had been hiding all this time. The mother and the daughter.

"If they are guests like you say, shouldn't they have left long ago?" I asked with a newfound confidence. "Clearly they have overstayed their welcome."

"Who told you that?" Grandma asked, immediately sensing that these were not my words.

"Fa... ther," I stammered. "I heard them talking this morning. Mother agrees with him."

"Does she?" Grandma said, a weariness in her voice. "And your father, is this how I raised him? In our culture we believe every guest is sent by God. We never ask guests to leave–they go when they are ready to go. That's the custom."

I knew all about our customs and I thought it was stupid and pointless to be talking about them now. Grandma needed to understand that the old ways were no longer pertinent. The earth was dying. The richest of the rich of each country had formed an international alliance to plan their escape to another planet. They had finally managed to put aside national, ethnic, historical conflicts. The wealthy were a nation of their own. With injections and supplements and pesticide-free diets, none of which were available to the general public, they were determined to live two hundred years–but first they had to get away from here, away from us.

There were so many rumors going around that it was hard to know what to believe anymore. My friends at school were convinced that the rich were going to hold a lottery someday soon, a contest to choose a few lucky citizens to take with them on their trip to another planet. I hated the thought of them climbing happily into their spaceships, excited to start everything anew. What were they going to do on their brand-new planet up there when billions of us were still stuck down here, trying, failing, fighting? Across the world, there were a few islands of prosperity left. And then vast expanses of poverty and growing misery. Inequality. Injustice. It boiled my blood, but what was worse was this sense of helplessness.

I hated feeling this way.

Death. Destruction. Decay. Every day there was a new calamity to worry about, another reason to fear the future. Lakes vanished, glaciers melted down, plants and animals became extinct, the weather... oh, the mighty weather, ticking like a metronome in the background, reminding us that it was always there, watching, biding its time. Only this year millions of climate refugees had been added to the existing ones– they slept out on the streets, camped in parks or parking lots or even cemeteries...

Preachers. Imams. Gurus. Mentors. The faster the change and the bigger the chaos, the more religious people seemed to become. Orators on every digital platform, pontificating and prattling! They spoke well, though, words dark and heavy as river stones. The most fanatical among them kept telling us that the end was nigh and what did we expect given that we had erred so badly for so long and now it was too late and we all had to repent, repent.

I was not going to do that. My generation was not responsible for this mess. I just wanted to live a decent, normal life. Was that too much to ask?

"You are angry," Grandma said.

And although I pretended not to hear, I knew she was right.

Growing up, I had heard many stories about the orchard. Golden apples so juicy and plentiful that hundreds would rot on the ground untouched; pomegranates, berries, figs, oranges, and cherries bright as ribbons; a large, lush vegetable garden with water gushing through roots; flower beds humming with bees... I had never seen it myself. It was all gone by the time I was born. Swept down in torrents of rain, scorched by the rays of sun. But these weren't the first ones to vanish from sight. It was the birds. It was them.

Grandma said that you know the earth is in trouble the day you look up at the sky and see not a single bird.

When I was younger I used to wonder where the birds had traveled to die. I asked Father one day. He smiled with an impatient toss of his head, his face clouding over as it always did when he didn't know what to say. In the end, he explained that birds–not unlike humans–died mostly of old age, while some died of broken hearts. He said they had passed out wherever they happened to be in that particular moment–up in the trees or down in the bushes–but we humans did not notice their remains because other animals quickly gobbled them up. Cats, for instance. I was not satisfied with this explanation. I should have asked Grandma. She might have answered it differently.

Guests. There were so many of them now in Istanbul. Nobody knew the exact number. Millions. Women, men, children. People who had lost their lands, livelihoods, memories. People who had witnessed things no human being should witness. Some of them tried to travel to Europe, taking enormous risks. If the waters of the Mediterranean Sea or the Aegean Sea or the Black Sea did not kill them, the walls did. Europa, like a medieval citadel, had surrounded itself with fortress walls, walls that had been custom-made in China and shipped in massive tankers across continents.

Why did I resent the stranger and her daughter? That wasn't my feeling when I first saw them at our door, months ago, a dying woman, a starving child, mere bones and skin, so battered you couldn't fathom right away how young the mother was, how beautiful the child; their dark eyes large, fearful, but gentle, always gentle. That wasn't my feeling when, one cold night last January, the child was running a fever and Grandma tried everything, every oil, each herb, to soothe the fire burning her forehead, and finally, after hours of wet towels and vinegar baths, finally, toward dawn, she uttered a word in her own language and we knew she would survive.

But fear. There is too much of it everywhere. It is in the air we inhale; it is in the heat that builds all day long; it is in the words we say to each other and the silences that stretch in between. I can't help noticing. Children are good at sensing their parents' fears.

"There is no East and West anymore," said Father once. "There is no North and South either. No left and right, not even that. The only distinction is between those who still have a bit of hope–and all the others."

Outside a streetlamp had been turned on, even though it was too early in the day. Waste of money, really. But I knew, and had learned not to question, that it was the duty of WeAreThePeople to decide the right time to switch on the streetlamps, just as it was his duty to make all decisions concerning his citizens' lives. After passing a law through the Parliament to dissolve the Parliament under the new state of EECE (Extreme Extended Climate Emergency), our president had officially changed his name to WeAreThePeople. Since then the people of our country had been called ThePresident. This way, WeAreThePeople ruled over ThePresident, and that was a good thing, a sign of a benevolent regime, we had been told.

Under EECE, voters had been regimented and ranked according to age, education, and status. Not everyone's vote had the same weight. Citizens above sixty-five were given a purple vote–the highest. But the more educated they happened to be, the more points they lost (high school degree, minus one; university degree, minus two; master's degree, minus three; doctorate and above, minus five), moving from a deep purple to a pale lavender.

"The uneducated ThePresidents are the real owners of this country," said WeAreThePeople. "And they should be the ones who determine what happens to it in this emergency."

Those who had been to high school or, worse, university, and those who had been reading books for a long time, had been brainwashed to such an extent that they had internalized values in conflict with our national and traditional values. As a result, they could not be trusted, even though they might be nice individuals in their hearts.

Those between the ages of forty-one and fifty-nine were given a bright blue vote, but then again, depending on their lack of education, they could earn extra points. My generation held a neon-green vote–regardless of diploma, which I always thought was unfair because God knows I would have loved to drop out of school right away. But a few years ago WeAreThePeople had restructured the whole education system and, now that the curriculum had been rewritten with the right values in mind, my generation was encouraged and expected to go to school.

Ethnic minorities enjoyed a yellow vote and sexual minorities a gray one–the lowest. Even so, there could be further variations up and down the social ladder. For instance, someone who had both an ethnic and a sexual minority would have a white vote, which contained barely any points. The votes of eighteen homosexuals from ethnic minority backgrounds equaled the vote of an elderly citizen from an ethnic majority background. If the former all happened to be university graduates and the latter was not, then the math had to be done again.

Democracy was complicated.

Refugees had no votes. "They should be grateful," said WeAreThePeople, "that we have taken them in."

"Ada, listen to me," said Grandma, bringing me back from my thoughts. "I don't want to see you angry. Especially at our guests."

"Can you stop calling them that? They are not *guests*. Why do we have to share our food with strangers when we don't have enough for ourselves?" My voice dropped.

"We have enough."

What I wanted to tell her was, *I heard Father and Mother talking. They sounded worried that we don't have food for this month*. But I heard myself utter something else instead: "They don't even speak our language."

"True, they don't," Grandma conceded. "That goes both ways. We don't speak theirs either."

"Father says it's dangerous to keep them any longer. If we get caught we'll be in trouble with the authorities. They must go back to where they came from."

A shadow crossed Grandma's face. "Where they came from there is nothing. Only hunger. Now, be a good girl and tell your Anger you accept its presence and it's fine if it wants to hang around for a bit, but you refuse to be ruled by it. Talk to your Anger."

"Tell me about bumblebees," I asked, hoping to change the subject.

If she was in a good mood, and she usually was, Grandma talked about the flowers of her youth. Animals she had taken care of or admired from a distance. Sometimes she told me about insects, too... I could not fathom how much of it was real and how much of it a figment of her imagination, stories from behind Mount Qaf. Not that I suspected she would try to deceive me, but it was highly possible that old age was playing tricks on her mind.

Mother disagreed with me. She believed Grandma had the memory of an elephant. Of ten elephants.

I had never seen one—an elephant, I mean. The zoo had been shut down long ago. Animals required a lot of water. And water we didn't have anymore. In a country surrounded by water on three sides, in a city built on water and always in flux, in a neighborhood nestled in the shadow of an ancient aqueduct, in a street named after a fountain... we had no water.

WeAreThePeople said our great nation would soon be able to make drinkable water out of seawater and alternative kinds of food out of remaining plants. If we only believed in ourselves and remembered the golden age many centuries ago when we had been victorious, and all our enemies had been shaking in their boots, if we could restore the confidence and the grandeur we possessed back then, we would do alright for ourselves. But before that we needed to control the flow of refugees—those coming in and those going out. We needed to keep them in check. Every outsider had to be reported to the police. Then the police would report them to the Ministry of Unknown Aliens, where they would be filed, photographed, and fingerprinted. After that they would be taken to refugee camps across the country, though everyone knew there were ways to escape those camps. In the meantime, WeAreThePeople would make calls to European politicians and negotiate with them. In return for each refugee we did not send to Europe, though we surely could anytime, we received a barrel of water from Europe.

"The bumblebees were amazing," said Grandma. "But you know what was even more fascinating? Fireflies! Tiny little lamps flying in the air on warm summer evenings. Now that was something!"

That night in my bed, I thought about fireflies. I wished I could have seen one. At least one single firefly.

But there were no fireflies left. Nor bumblebees. Instead I had anxieties and fears perching on my shoulders, buzzing around my ears. There was so little I could control in this world, too much uncertainty. It occurred to me that tomorrow morning after breakfast I could go to the police and inform them that we were hiding two refugees in the basement of our house. Mother would be relieved and, secretly, Father too. I could do it quietly. I would be back home before noon. No one would know.

But as soon as the thought hit me I felt a burning sense of shame. Grandma's unseeing eyes pierced holes into my soul. *Talk to your Anger.*

In the distance I heard a strange sound carried on the wind and for a moment it felt like the recordings I'd heard of the seagull's call, the notorious lodos that Istanbul had once been known for. Maybe there were still a few birds out there. Maybe they had not all died. Grandma was right. I needed to learn to calm down. The noises inside my head slowed down, shushing, swirling, fading, until there remained only a sigh.

Somewhere in the house was Grandma hunched over her prayer rug, thumbing her amber rosary, her unseeing eyes turned toward the skies, and there were my parents whispering in their bed upstairs, their fingers touching and their breaths mixing less out of passion than out of a need for familiarity. Somewhere in the house was also a little child who spoke only in her dreams or when ill with fever, uttering words in another language, and next to her a young mother, probably awake, listening to the night for signs of danger. They had no one left in this world, only us. And perhaps it was also the other way around, or very soon it would be. We did not have much left in this world either, only them.

I didn't realize that I had been crying until I felt the tears roll down my face onto the pillow. Darkness grew all around me, thicker and denser but also softer now, wrapping me like a warm velvet cloak, and I knew that I no longer wanted to feel angry like this. I no longer wanted to feel anxious like this.

We were all here, somewhere in this house, in this city, in this earth. We had no one but each other.

MCS58

30°03'12.8"N

GHOST TOWN
by Kanishk Tharoor

IN HER YOUNGER DAYS, KAMALA Devi reveled in the smell of the onion fields in moonlight. She'd sneak out of her home to meet friends, cousins, boys, and eventually the young man who became her husband. Early on, Yash had taken her by the waist and lowered her beneath the hum of the insects. That sudden movement, so decisive and forceful, surprised her and surprised Yash as well, and they lay amid the onions, his body rigid with fear, barely daring to move his lips from where they rested on her cheek. It was left to her to remove the glasses from his face and guide his mouth. She remembered that it was nearing harvest time that night. White and lilac petals drooped from the wilting onion stalks. As Yash nuzzled her breasts with his nose, she found herself imagining water coursing through the roots, up into the great reservoir of the bulb, where it seethed and tumbled, a river pulsing between the walls of the onion, frothing up through the stem until it met the air in an umbel of flowers.

But the older she got, the more perverse that smell seemed to her, too thick and insistent. Bipin, their only child, became fed up with his parents' attachment to the village and their onion field. He had grown sick of scrabbling in the moun-tains. Every so often, the incomprehensible heat of the plains would reach up, a scorching taste of what was happening below. The villagers were all bemused, incredulous that the nightmarish temperatures of the lowlands could rise this close to the clouds. But what seemed a freak occurrence became typical. The rains began to fail, coming later and later in the year as the crops wilted in the dust. "Don't you see, Ma?" he would say. "We also can't stay." The villages in the foothills and the towns in the plains had already emptied. Under pressure from the unbearable heat, whole lowland clans–families that had survived in the region for as long as anybody knew–upped sticks to squat under bridges and overpasses in cities far away. Up in their mountains, not only was it harder to grow onions, there was nobody to sell them to. Everybody in their village had the same problem. There was a shrinking market, and little money to be made. Bipin looked despairingly at their struggling plot. All his cousins, all his friends, all the morose uncles, all the muscular aunts, all of them had gone. The night before he left, Bipin fought with Kamala Devi and Yash, and tried to convince them to move with him like sensible people. In the morning, Yash wept at the sight of his son in trousers, a burlap bag on his shoulder. Kamala Devi asked Bipin to send what money he could, but not to sacrifice for them; he should live his life fully, he was doing the right thing.

"Why won't you leave, Ma, why won't you leave?" Bipin was disconsolate.

"There's the house," she said, as if their one-room dwelling with its tin roof and windows patched with plastic were an immovable argument. And she nodded in the direction of the field. "There are the onions."

Bipin inhaled. He marveled at the stubbornness of his parents–sometimes, the older we get, the more impermanent the world seems, the more things can be changed, matters altered. But not here. "Promise you'll come during the holidays," Yash said. Bipin promised he would and left with the rising of the mist.

Within months, they received word that Bipin had fallen from a high scaffold, across the sea in Oman, and died.

The village was so empty then that only five others accompanied them in performing the funerary rites. In the absence of a priest–he was supposed to come from a nearby town, but never showed up–they muddled through and improvised as best they could. Yash fretted that they had done an insufficient job, that their son hadn't properly been sent off. Kamala Devi didn't have the strength to disagree; she had fooled herself for years believing she was one of the lucky mothers who would never have to let their child go.

The thought of leaving grew even more distant. Former neighbors and distant relatives all urged them to come down from the mountains, to leave the village behind. But leave to go where? Leave to go to whom? Should they wander the desolate plains, make a tour of the ghost towns? Like everybody else, should they jostle for space in the big cities, where they would unroll their mats in the alleys of a shantytown, beg for water, steal into a shop for a kiss of air conditioning? No, they wouldn't. When their last neighbor left, they roamed up and down the path as if in a daze, wondering if a village without people was still a village. But their solitude was not something to fear or regret. What world could there be for them beyond their own? It didn't seem right that they might live elsewhere, that without ever wanting it for themselves they might live a life denied to their son.

The monkeys came into the onion field only at night, out of respect for their vocation as thieves. It was too brazen, even for them, to rummage for bulbs during the day. By the time the sun rose, the monkey clan had wandered back to the trees, whispering to each other and passing onion gruel into the mouths of their babies. Kamala Devi limped out of the cottage and thought for an instant that all was well, that nothing had happened in the night. The field was gray and shapeless, as gray and shapeless as she had left it at dusk. But then she stepped on broken stalks and spotted tufts of hair on the ground where two monkeys had wrestled, and she realized that she had allowed herself to be robbed yet again.

It was the third time in so many weeks. Kamala Devi had raised onions all her life, and never before had they invited the persistent ravages of monkeys. The withdrawal of so many humans from the village had emboldened them. She scolded the scarecrow. "Why didn't you stop them," she said, "always just standing there doing nothing... You're useless." The scarecrow swayed slightly at the reproach, aggrieved, as if to say: *What do you take me for, a scaremonkey?* Annoyed, she stripped the scarecrow of its hat and thwacked it on the arm. The dew sparkled in the sunlight, showing Kamala Devi the patches where the monkeys had performed their most committed excavations. She calculated the loss in terms of packets of biscuits and cups of tea, and concluded that she might have to go a week without her afternoon sweet. In truth, it was a miracle they had even this many onion bulbs growing. For as long as she could remember, the villagers would scan the skies a month or two before the rainy season. If they saw thick clouds high in the sky, they divined that there would be a very wet season ahead; if the clouds were sparse and lower, it wouldn't rain as much. That perception determined when they would plant the onions. With the rains becoming more erratic, and with the high temperatures changing cloud patterns, it became next to impossible to figure out the right time to plant. These onions relied on prayers, on luck, on the instincts of an old couple raking the soil with hope and fear.

Kamala Devi looked at the forest sloping up from her plot of land, mist hanging from the trees, a cloud settling on the wreck of a once-hopeful signal tower. Somewhere in the rousing green of the valley, there were monkeys making a rogue breakfast from her onions.

She replaced the hat on the scarecrow, suddenly feeling a bit sad for its threadbare pate. It wore a ragged sweatshirt that her son had left behind and never returned for. Yash called from the cottage to ask for hot coals for his hookah. She hobbled to the brazier at the front of their home, where a few embers still burned low. Up and down the main path, every window was boarded up, every door padlocked, every wall peeling. The only life in the hamlet was in their home, where her husband Yash scratched himself in the doorway and knelt over the hookah to prepare his morning smoke.

"The damn monkeys," she told her husband, "please do something about them." Yash lifted his face upwards to the clouds, from where all his wife's requests seemed to descend. "What can I do about monkeys?" His voice was vaporous, not yet thickened to its usual fog. She plucked the glasses from his face and began to rub them with the end of her aanchal.

"They're eating our onions," she said. "I won't have it." He blinked at her and his enormous Adam's apple shifted mutely. He looked at his hands.

"I couldn't kill them," he said. She shook her head in agreement. It went without saying that nobody else would kill them either. Some years ago, there were still people living in their village, people of various ages, little boys who might be tempted to patrol the fields with sticks for the promise of a few coins. The labor of others was now a remote idea, almost unfathomable to Kamala Devi and Yash in their isolation. If the facts of the world could be changed, only they would change them.

Monkeys were a difficult kind of fact. Farmers across the region had a range of techniques for keeping the creatures away. There were chemicals that you could spray around the border fences. Poorer farmers used dried fish instead, which drove monkeys to such madness that they would rub themselves until they bled. The poorest farmers rolled balls of rice in heaps of chili powder and sprinkled them around the edges of the field. Scathed, their tongues on fire, the monkeys would retreat to forage elsewhere.

Kamala Devi and Yash could not afford any of these defenses. They rarely ever had enough rice for themselves, never mind the laying of spicy landmines. Pesticides had been used in the village in the past, but were now entirely out of reach, both too expensive and too far away. With no neighbors to borrow from, Yash would have to walk over fifteen kilometers to the nearest village, where he'd catch a sporadic bus to the market town, where he'd have to hope that the old vendor was still there. And if by some miracle that merchant had remained in his empty town, would he remember Yash and sell the chemicals on credit? Kamala Devi didn't begrudge her husband avoiding this unlikely quest.

They didn't have dried fish either, nor did either of them have the wherewithal to catch fish in the high streams. In any case, Kamala Devi found something horrific in the thought of incensed monkeys scratching themselves raw under the flowering stalks of her onions.

Instead, wife and husband settled on devising a ruse. Kamala Devi recalled a practice from the next valley, where farmers once dangled multicolored rubber hoses around their fields. The hoses would hang like snakes on a branch, stirring in the mind of an invading monkey a deep, immemorial fear.

Of course, Yash and Kamala Devi didn't have spare hoses themselves.

"Perhaps there are old hoses in the neighbors' homes," she said. Yash squatted and flexed his toes with their black and blue nails.

"We shouldn't steal," he said. Kamala Devi sighed, at once annoyed and warmed by her husband's loyal melancholy.

"We're just borrowing them… After the harvest, you can put them back."

They spent the rest of the morning scavenging. Yash approached their neighbors' homes politely, as if he were an unwanted guest. Though padlocked, many doors had rusted off their hinges and it was just a matter of pushing. In other places, they could open the shutters and clamber through the windows. It was odd picking over the remains of their neighbors' belongings. To be fair, both of them had done this several times in previous years, in search of tobacco or medicines or spoons. But it never ceased to feel like a violation. On his way out of a dust-filled home where birds sparred under the shingles, Yash apologized to a doorpost.

His wife rummaged farther down the path. It was hot and humid, and Yash longed for the gentle summers of his youth, months that felt infinite in their warmth, the frosts of winter forgotten. Now, the clouds assembled beneath the peaks and blew sudden wet winds, but they didn't break with rain. There was no respite. The sun broke through again like a hammer. Yash leaned against a wobbly fence and inhaled the thick air. It bothered him that he no longer remembered exactly which house belonged to which family. When the village was full, or even half-full, neighbors were to be gossiped about and lamented. How loud she plays her radio, must they complain about the heat all the time, he lets his goat eat our spinach, she stares at me with such jealous eyes, why do they have to dress their children so well, it makes the rest of us look bad. In their absence, Yash felt sorry for all the times he had spoken ill of them to his wife, all those moments when his wife, peering out the window, would shake her head and snort. If they hadn't been so snide–even in secret–perhaps some of the others might have stayed.

Kamala Devi's search turned up three rubber hoses, all in ratty condition, but they would pass as snakes. With the lines slung over her back, she struggled onto the path and called to Yash for help. He did not answer. She called out again. For a moment she entertained the helpless fantasy of being truly alone. But it was an articulated silence, the kind of silence she was sensitive to after decades of life together, a silence in which she felt his blood moving. She came to a doorway and saw him squatting inside the front room of somebody's abandoned home, holding a hairbrush.

"What happened?" she asked and dabbed at the tears slipping down the creases of his face. Yash looked at her with his mouth open, gulping a sob.

"Don't you remember this brush?" Kamala Devi did remember it. For some people, a lifetime of hairbrushes may hardly be worth the space of their remembering, but for Yash and Kamala Devi, the objects they gained and kept were fairly precious. Each was more than just an instrument; it was a kind of claim to belonging in the world, which up in their mountains could otherwise seem so tenuous and on the verge of dissolving.

It had been her hairbrush years before, a chip of the plastic missing from the handle. When she managed to get a replacement, Bipin had taken it. He picked every last strand of hair from its bristles and gave it to the girl who lived in this now empty house. Kamala Devi remembered her son's return from gifting the girl this brush, the shy hidden smile, how he couldn't control the energy of his limbs. She had sent him to tend to the field. With the sun setting, she'd watched Bipin skip around the onion rows, swatting away invisible enemies with a stick, each thin motion of his body brimming with laughter.

Kamala Devi released Yash's fingers from the brush and enfolded her husband in her arms.

*   *   *

The human village once glowed with the light of many lives. Now it is dark and empty. From the perspective of the monkeys, there seems to be little dividing the hamlet from the surrounding hills. The jungle has already retaken those houses on the outskirts, their fields and gardens, once so militantly kept, now overgrown. A few homes are topless, roofs caved in. Blackness calls through the windows. Only in one place, at the heart of the village, are there humans. The light of a gas lamp struggles to reach out of the door and onto the ambling back of an old female. She picks through the lines of her crop, fingering the green shoots. The monkeys watch her without making a sound. She straightens and looks at the stars, the dull moon, and, many valleys away, the faintest haze of other humans. When she returns to her home, the monkeys wait for the lamp to be blown out. Then the order is given, the parents release their grips on the tails of the young, and the whole troop comes out of the forest, alive to the sweet, perverse smell of onions.

Later, up in the trees, one monkey hoards his cache of onion shoots. Others soon notice that he has not consumed his share. They pester him, chucking old fruit in his direction, besieging him with suggestions. When dealing with their own kind, most monkeys, like most humans, are good-natured, and see force as a means of last resort. They try to persuade him. You can't possibly eat so much, they explain, why keep all those onions to yourself? He bats them away and climbs to a higher branch. You look ridiculous, they say, you can't even swing properly, what with those onions clutched between your hands and feet, squeezed under your armpits. He snarls at them and attempts to move to another tree, but encumbered as he is, he stumbles, and his onions fall to the ground. Monkeys below whoop with glee and gather them up to feast.

Chastened, he retreats higher, to the canopy, holding with two hands the only onion left to him. The bulb is young and tough, the shoot thin. It will hardly do, he thinks, what a terrible gift. All creatures have powers of imagination, and with his, he has dreamt of impressing the young monkey he wants as his mate; he will give her a stack of onions. He thrusts his head above the line of leaves and branches, feels the sunlight cut through his eyes and drum on the top of his head. He cannot fight for her; he has a modest and wholly self-aware sense of his chances. Other monkeys are bigger, other monkeys are stronger, other monkeys delight in the pell-mell of the scrum. But perhaps with a significant donation, she might look at him with her watery eyes, turn her back, and let him lift up her tail.

He eats the onion, which is hard like a pebble. Tonight, he resolves, tonight I will forage for my mate.

He leads the assault. The other monkeys are surprised by his bravado; normally he's more the shrinking sort. But the moon is a sliver and the stars are drowsy and for once the darkness doesn't mock the monkeys with its terrors but resolves around them like armor. He can smell the onions now and picks up the pace, a battalion scampering and clambering behind him.

The dangling form of a rubber hose gives him only a moment's pause. He studies its length, and cannot see its head, concluding that it is probably a vine or some kind of creeper, not a python. He turns and calls out to his companions. Watch out for the snakes! This will slow them down, he thinks, more onions for me.

The human female has abandoned her post and gone off inside her dwelling. The monkey knows the scarecrow isn't real: some kind of frozen, immobile, perfectly useless being. He rolls into the line of crops. The earth smells wet and he presses his nose to the ground and hears the thrum of water coursing and insects shifting and faintly, almost imperceptible but still loud enough to the monkey, the sighs of onions growing old. He begins to dig. The treasures come out one by one, white heads with long green beards and the dreadlocks of roots. He amasses them in a pile. Other monkeys arrive nearby. Such a liar, they call to him, you can't have this field all to yourself.

They grow silent. He sees a human foot. It is attached to a human leg, and another leg, and then the whole body of a man moves through the onion field. The monkey backs away, scrambling for his onions. He notices a powerful absence: the human has no smell.

The human glows. When the monkey summons the courage to look up, the human's face is a dark swirling cloud, smoke and vapor. But then it gathers, hardening into the face of a young man with very white teeth and plump eyebrows. He looks down on the monkey and smiles. With impossible speed, the young man's arm swings downwards, and the monkey feels the hand pass through his chest like a cold wind.

The other monkeys yell and flee back to the forest. Again, the man's head turns into a black nimbus, bolts of lightning flashing around its edges, and the monkey feels himself rising as if lifted by a gale that brings him level with the man's cloud-head. A boy's face emerges from the murk. What kind of human is this? the monkey begins to think, but can no more, his monkey mind overwhelmed with a flood of human images and smells: bread forked straight out of a tandoor, a father wetting and combing the boy's hair, a mother massaging his little feet with eucalyptus oil, the parted lips of a girl, fireworks in a bright village, the damp of the onion field under a full moon, a desert–unfathomable to the monkey, but now so clear–with dunes wavering away to the horizon, a tree of steel beams and scaffolds, and then the broken harness and slipped line, and the shattering fall that the monkey feels now as an echo, a ripple of some distant and immense pain reaching up and down his hairy body.

He tumbles to the floor and without looking back runs to the forest. When at last his panic releases him, the monkey climbs up a tree and gazes down on the field. He cannot see any human there, only the motionless form of the scarecrow. Even monkeys can experience wonder. He hangs from the branch, staring over the forest, uncertain if he'll ever want an onion again.

Yash rose before Kamala Devi that morning. She had tossed and turned during the night and, without meaning to, slept in long after sunrise. She blinked awake to find her husband standing over her with a cup of tea. "Come," he said, "I want to show you something." He led her outside. Kamala Devi could already sense that the monkeys had visited again in the night, that the rubber snakes had failed. But there was a lightness in Yash's manner that made her curious.

He guided her into the center of the field. "Look." He pointed down near the base of the scarecrow.

"I'm hardly awake, what is it?" she said.

"Look, just look." He squeezed her wrist and they knelt by the pile of dug-up onions. After all the nights of wanton pillage, the monkeys had simply abandoned their loot. Kamala Devi laughed. If this is how the world repays me for my patience, she thought, so be it. She moved to sweep up the decorous onion mound, but Yash gasped. "No," he said, and stopped her, as if she were about to disturb something sacred, a strange gift from another world.

1740
by Asja Bakić

(Translated by Jennifer Zoble)

I'M SITTING ON MY FRONT patio. Drenched in sweat. The last time Vilko came by he left me some deodorant and insect repellent, but I use both sparingly. The sweat from my armpits reminds me of the literature I read to make the days shorter. Sappy love stories, occasionally Dostoevsky (which causes me to sweat from discomfort), and rarely, when I can summon the strength, natural history, stories about animals, about bygone eras and extinct species. I sweat the most from those books, but I pretend the sweat is from the heat and humidity. I even pretend for Vilko, and I've known him for years. While she was still alive, my mother used to say she had no time for books because there were better things to do. As a result, I didn't like reading either, but now I have all the time in the world. I need to spend it somehow.

Humans aren't quite an extinct species from the distant past, but they are endangered by their efforts to survive at all costs. People can survive anything and everything, but if I were to spend the whole day enumerating exactly what they can survive, I'd probably die from sheer agony. Instead I stick my head in a book and pretend that, at moments like these, it makes sense. I don't want to ruminate, so

I read. I devour letters. A little drop of sweat trickles down my cheek. I say it's a drop of sweat, but of course I'm lying. Lying helps me survive–it's because of lying that I'm not an extinct species myself. I've been lying my entire life. I don't know exactly what I'm reading–a historical lie, descriptions of the prosperity in some glorious past, something about the Western Roman Empire. Petronius' *Satyricon*? The letters look blurry; I'm sweating so much I can no longer see them clearly. Big drops fall onto the paper. I wipe my eyes with a cloth from the side table. Before I can continue reading, I hear the sound of a motor–it's Vilko's boat making its way to my house. No one else visits me, only him and sometimes Višnja, his wife. Vilko tries to persuade me to take my boat over to their place, but I'm a rat who jumped ship to survive. The floods drove me away to my cabin. Once in a while I go to the city to buy supplies, and then I retreat home, to continue shortening my life with literature as much as I possibly can. I mostly lounge on the patio, which gives me a view of the other cabins and the garbage dump close to our neighborhood. No one bothers to cover the garbage anymore because the water carries it off regardless. Right now, there's a rainbow over the dump. I stare at it. I need to look at something to calm down.

Vilko approaches from the left, but I keep staring straight ahead. I throw the dirty, wet cloth on the floor. I don't throw it, really, I drop it, but I like to pretend I'm doing things consciously, making an effort. When Vilko cuts the motor, I can hear the waves lapping lightly against the improvised dock where he quickly and silently ties up the boat. From the corner of my eye I can see he's carrying a crate of something, but I don't get up to help him. I don't go to greet him. I hate people, even those I consider friends. Vilko hastily climbs onto the patio.

"You're crying again?" he asks.

He never beats around the bush. Maybe that's why I still consider him a friend.

"It's sweat," I lie. "It's hot."

I have a headache. Vilko rests the crate at my feet. Inside there's a loaf of bread, a bit of lard, milk. Underneath them something else, but I don't lift the kitchen towel Višnja covered the food with for protection from flies. I note only what's visible. What I can count on.

"Višnja says hi," says Vilko.

I'm silent. I'm sure he made that up.

"She couldn't come because she's working, but she made you a cake and some dandelion honey."

"Where'd she find dandelions?" I ask, surprised.

"At the market, from the woman she always buys from."

Humans lie to survive, as I've already stated, but I repeat, they lie and lie, and most of all to themselves. And now Vilko's standing here and lying about Višnja's shopping place, which has nothing to do with what we used to call a market. I look at him and hold back my thoughts. I don't want sweat to roll down my cheeks again. My eyes itch and I rub them nervously. I know they're red.

"Don't cry," says Vilko.

He never says anything to console me, only to soothe himself. If my tears flow then his will, too: maybe not now, but when he's sitting again in his boat and heading home, he'll start to cry. He'll admit to himself there's no more market, that Višnja bought the dandelions in a place that bears no resemblance to one. The monoculture farming systems that feed us don't need markets. He's aware of that. If Vilko isn't crying now, it just means that he cried earlier, before he came over.

"Višnja sent you a book," he says, rummaging through the crate.

He pushes a volume into my hands. I look at what he's given me. Nina Epton, *Love and the French*.

"*Love and the French*. I have this."

"That's a shame," Vilko says.

"Where'd she get it?" I ask.

"The same woman she bought the dandelions from."

I don't give the book back.

"This one's in better shape than mine. Thank her."

I can see he's glad I'm keeping it.

"She knows you love that theme, and the eighteenth century."

"Višnja knows everything," I say.

Vilko nods, but I'm sure he's bothered by my cynical tone. He sits in the chair next to mine, even though I haven't offered it. We're old friends—he doesn't need to ask.

"She also found some books on the history of prostitution, but the covers were damp, so she didn't take them."

"That would be too many books at once."

"I know, but she says you have a lot of catching up to do since you didn't read before the warming."

"As I said, your Višnja knows everything."

I've purposely thrown in *your* to see how Vilko will react, but nothing. We sit in silence. I look at his and Višnja's boat. They've renamed it again. First, they wrote VIŠNJA on it, but then they repainted it and wrote ALBERTINA. Now it just says BOAT.

"You can't decide on a name?"

"Albertina was a nice name, but I wasn't sure this clunker deserved it."

"But Boat?"

"That was Višnja's idea."

"Of course," I say.

"You know her and her sense of humor."

"It's always been terrible," I say.

We stare at the garbage dump. I know we can't spend the whole time talking about Višnja. It remains to be seen which one of us will have the guts to bring up the real reason for Vilko's visit. I can go out for food on my own. This is about something bigger, something much more important. Vilko's leg is furiously shaking. That always happens when he's nervous. He needs time to gather his thoughts. I'm expecting some complaint, but he surprises me. His voice is excited, almost joyful.

"I think we're close," he says. "Just a couple more weeks and the device will be finished."

"Are you joking?"

"Višnja worked on the program all night. That's why she didn't come with me. Fink and Gmaz are with her. We're almost there."

"Are you sure?"

I can't believe my ears.

"The code you rewrote works."

I don't know what to say. I recall the lines I wrote on a piece of greasy paper Višnja had used to wrap a slab of bacon. My strokes were a sort of calligraphy, but those lines of code, casually recorded, were like the name Albertina: pretty, but completely inappropriate for the situation in which we've found ourselves. I don't know where I got the inspiration. These days I hardly ever turn on the computer. I didn't want to spend all my time staring at the program Gmaz and Višnja had written. It struck me as crude, in the same way the flooded Balkans do: pearls scattered here and there, and everything else swirling in the fetid water with trash floating on its surface. I peer at that water now, stunned. I don't know what I'm feeling. The floods and the computer program both are the product of human hands. How can we make such lovely and such disgusting things at the same time?

Vilko doesn't push me to speak. He knows I'm in shock. I've fixed my gaze on the red buoy that a relative of mine sent in a package along with a fishing net, a fishing rod, and some bait. The water level is higher than ever before, and I often awake in terror from the murmur. I fear the level will quietly rise until the surf drowns all of us in our sleep. The question is whether I managed to fix Gmaz's part of the code because I was terrified, as I first claimed to Višnja, or because I wanted to regain a false sense of control at all costs. I gaze at the buoy and the water as if I'm seeing far into the future. I avoid my reflection: the only thing more horrible than the flooding is the human face. My thoughts wander and I don't know what to say. I don't want to contemplate Vilko's words. They're too significant. I think instead about how I never enjoyed going to the sea, and now it comes right up to my house. And I can't even fish–there are practically no more fish. The fishing gear flung on the patio serves only to remind me of this. There's no point in throwing them away because I know everything I discard will float right back to my front door. People can no longer hide their mistakes anywhere.

"I didn't think it would work," I say to Vilko after the long silence. "I was convinced it wouldn't."

Before the flooding, I worked with Višnja and Vilko at the Ruđer Bošković Institute. I was a theoretical physicist, but I also did programming on the side because my parents loved money and wanted me to love it just as much.

"You're too prone to abstraction," my mother said.

She wanted me to study economics and management.

"The money's in the money," she added.

My father agreed.

"As long as she doesn't study the humanities," my mother declared to the family while making rakija.

Traditional values had always mattered in the Balkans. My parents were no exception. Family, money, and rakija. Rakija was always made at our house, at the cabin where I was ultimately forced to live alone. I've often thought about our long-lost fruit trees. Plum, pear, apple. And especially the cherry tree. The entire supply of rakija my parents had kept in the attic for my wedding, I sat drinking on this patio, out of my mind with fear of drowning. One can still find potable water, but there's no more rakija. My parents come to mind from time to time, but alcohol is there constantly. In truth, the memory of rakija compelled me, sweaty and tired, to write code on the greasy paper. I've missed it something awful. The cemetery where my parents were buried is underwater. The Balkans are underwater. The only thing keeping my head above it is the memory of višnjevača, the rakija that's sweet and tart all at once, like life, like a human being. If the rakija is good, you never get a headache. I want to drink, forget everything, if only for a moment. I stare at the garbage dump day in day out. I stare at the consequences. I want to get away from them.

"How many of us can fit at the same time in the machine?" I ask Vilko.

"All five of us. Fink and Gmaz can sit in the back."

"There wasn't enough room for everyone before," I say.

"I know," Vilko replies, "but Višnja relocated the controls and removed a non-essential panel. If they squeeze in, they can both fit."

"And me?"

"There's always a space for you."

"Are you sure?" I ask.

Vilko looks at me. He senses my apprehension.

"Višnja won't oppose it. You helped her a lot with the code."

"I know, but..."

"No buts," says Vilko.

"There's always a but," I correct him. "Especially with Višnja."

I drank the last bit of rakija two years ago. I scoured the attic in hopes of finding a stray bottle, one that had perhaps rolled under my mother's old furniture, but there was nothing. Višnja and Vilko never drink–they want to be fully present, sober witnesses to the demise of the human race. They are far nobler people than I am. Science was supposed to be noble, but the ideas I worked on were so abstract that nobility didn't matter that much. Ideas simply existed. The idea of progress, for example. I'd always been in favor of progress. Exactly what kind of progress wasn't important. I just wanted to move forward. I didn't care about money quite as much as my parents wanted me to, but I loved having it all the same because money and progress were closely related. All of my abstract ideas were constrained by the reality of money.

I failed as a scientist, but succeeded as a programmer. I made money for others, and then for myself. I purchased real estate, invested in various funds and companies. I ultimately had so much money that my bank balance was completely unimaginable to Vilko and Višnja. That money wasn't earned through science, but it helped raise the air temperature by one and a half degrees Celsius, which ruined me. What had appeared abstract to people became very concrete when it began to affect their lives.

"When it began to affect *your* life," Višnja would correct me.

"I remember," I say to Vilko absentmindedly, "the cherry tree my parents had in front of the house. Its blossoms were so beautiful thanks to my father's diligent care. I miss that tree the most."

Vilko has heard this story so many times he knows it by heart, but he doesn't interrupt me. He can tell I'm falling into one of the nostalgic moods I won't be able to escape.

"It's hard to imagine it was there, just a few steps away from us. And look now!" I gesture toward the garbage dump.

"Look!"

"I'm looking," says Vilko, but he isn't.

Višnja was rather touched the first time I told her about my father and the tree, presumably because of the relation to her name, which means "cherry," but then she realized I was covertly drinking rakija from the attic and stopped coming to listen to my laments about better times.

"You don't care about the consequences of global warming," she once said angrily. "You're just sorry you can't drink yourself into oblivion with this swamp water we're surrounded by."

I didn't contradict her. After that Vilko continued to come on his own. He kept me apprised of their progress constructing the machine. I didn't resent Višnja. She rarely came by, only when she needed to ask me about some complicated detail. She'd consult me, I'd help her, but she'd never stick around. Not like Vilko sitting on the patio and watching the rainbow over the dump. Višnja had never been particularly sentimental. It was clear she'd never seek solace in alcohol. She couldn't understand me.

"It's still unbelievable to me," says Vilko, "that you managed to solve our biggest puzzle with that marker on greasy paper."

I told everyone I'd had a sudden burst of inspiration, but that, of course, was a lie. I'd in fact spent the entire day at the computer, biting my lower lip. I'd tinkered with Višnja's and Gmaz's code, which Vilko had brought with the insect repellent and deodorant. I saw the outline of Višnja's idea. I could clearly grasp the intention she'd casually imparted to me. She'd never wanted to show me all the software; she'd brought only those tricky parts she needed help with. She didn't trust me. I had just barely persuaded Vilko to copy the rest and bring it without Višnja's knowledge.

"I'm not sure that's a good idea," he had said at first.

"Of course it isn't, but you need my help."

He knew I was right. Fink and Vilko were engineers. Gmaz was a programmer, but he was incompetent. Višnja did anything and everything, just not as well as I did.

"You shouldn't tell her right away," I insisted to Vilko.

"I have to tell her, I never lie to her. Never."

"Fine, but tell her only when I've finished the code."

In the end he showed me sketches of the machine. Half of the construction had been done at the Institute, in secret, and the other half in Višnja's garage. That half had been made of parts stolen from Vojin Bakić's experimental monuments and sculptures.

"If they catch you destroying Bakić, you'll be out of work. Both of you," I said.

"His work has been destroyed before. They took the plaque from his monument at Petrova Gora, but nothing happened."

"That was before," I said. "Times are different now."

"We stole them for the greater good," Vilko said, attempting to justify himself.

For the greater good is such a tired phrase. Virtue, the greater good–stupid notions that even the literature I've been devouring of late doesn't portray as intelligent or inspiring. Goodness is overrated. Especially in the sciences. I, on the other hand, wanted to write the program to completion, my way, then hop into the machine and finally get out of here. My feelings warranted the travel that Višnja so greedily sought to reserve for herself and her friends.

"I'm giving you twenty-four hours," said Vilko, "and then I'm telling her I gave you a copy. Don't screw me over."

"I won't," I promised.

When I was very sad, and Vilko was nowhere in sight, I'd sit in my boat and ride around the settlement. The majority of my neighbors had left this area around Zagreb. I didn't know where they'd gone. A few remained. They'd been good friends of my late parents. Before the warming, everyone had grown identical gardens and orchards. They'd celebrated Christmas and Easter. Eaten turkey and mlince flatbread. Some of them had made bad wine, some honey, but most prepared homemade rakija in large pots. If there was anything the neighbors remembered my parents by, it was their rakija. But even mom's rakija didn't help with her bragging, which she tended to do often, particularly about how smart I was for not studying the humanities.

"She'll have money," she said.

What Mama didn't know was that I would have money but I wouldn't have a future. She couldn't connect those two things because she didn't trouble her mind with what wasn't directly in front of her. She couldn't understand that abstract ideas have concrete consequences.

"Money is heating up the environment," Višnja told my mother, but it was already too late.

Višnja was always in the first row at all the demonstrations. When birds began to die off, even the common species we'd taken for granted, she and Vilko were the first to write a protest letter to the Institute demanding that it support the Council of Environmental Protection.

"It needs more funding," they wrote.

MCS58

45°48'54.1"N

I mocked her at work.

"Didn't you say that money is the problem? And now you're seeking more?"

"Don't be cynical," she said.

But (the eternal but) I wanted to be a cynic. I was a cynic. It was a conscious decision. My character. I devoted myself to making snide comments to my colleagues and strangers on the internet. I didn't spare my handful of friends. I was my most cynical around them.

"You've gone silent again," Vilko says.

I forgot that I haven't answered him. My mind is racing with thoughts of the machine.

"Where did you put it?"

"Put what?" Vilko asks.

"The machine."

"In the garage. We have to hide it from the Institute."

"Can I see it?"

"Now?"

Vilko seems surprised. I've never asked to see it before.

"If it's not a problem. Do you want to check with Višnja?"

Vilko fumbles in his pocket nervously and retrieves his phone. He calls Višnja. I can't hear what she's saying.

"Višnja says it's too crowded in the garage at the moment, but you can come tomorrow."

"No problem," I say.

When Vilko leaves, I get into my boat and follow his. He's distracted and doesn't notice me trailing him. I shut off the motor to be quiet. He doesn't go to the garage or the Institute, but rather Gmaz's house. I recognize the facade. Fink opens the door for him. Before Vilko enters I see him kick away some garbage that's floated up to the door.

"You can't just read literature that makes you cry," Višnja tells me when I see her the next day.

"You're right," I say. "Sometimes I forget how sensitive I am."

"That's your mother's fault."

"The only thing you haven't blamed on her is global warming," I say.

"I wouldn't be wrong to blame her for that too. She laughed when I said she needed to sort her trash."

"She didn't know any better."

"Now her unsorted trash comes up to your cabin to haunt you," says Višnja. She's in a good mood.

"Thanks for the cake and honey," I say.

"Vilko said you already have the book about love."

"I do, but it's okay."

I don't want to talk about love, only about machines. Specifically one machine. As if she knows, Višnja doesn't bring it up. She talks about everything else just to avoid mentioning it. Luckily Gmaz has just returned with parts to install on the steering console. He's hoping to pass quickly through the kitchen, but I pose a question to him before he can get away.

"Is that part of the steering console for a motorboat?" I ask.

"Uh-huh," says Gmaz.

Neither he nor Fink is especially talkative. Compared to them I'm a chatterbox.

"Do you need help with that?"

I want to see the machine, and Višnja's never going to show it to me.

"You're not an engineer," he says.

Višnja doesn't say anything, but I can see her gripping the edge of a chair. I've spoiled her mood.

"Where's Vilko?" she asks Gmaz.

"In the garage," he replies. "Waiting for this part."

Gmaz lifts the console into the air. He holds it above his head long enough for me to make out the model number. I memorize it and follow him into the garage where the others are waiting. Before we're out of sight, I notice Višnja observing me carefully. Just as I've read the steering console, she's reading me. I feel like a piece of plastic garbage my mother stubbornly refused to sort while she was alive.

In the garage, Fink sits at the computer and meticulously reviews some calculation. Vilko connects wires inside the machine.

"I found it!" yells Gmaz.

"Well done!" says Fink.

Vilko just stretches out his hand, but Gmaz nevertheless places the console on the worktable.

"Višnja needs to inspect it first. We can't dismantle and install it just yet."

"You're right," says Vilko.

He gets out of the machine, and can't hide his surprise at seeing me.

"Višnja knows you're here?"

"We were just chatting in the kitchen."

"Then it's all right," Vilko says.

I sit down next to Fink. I'm interested in what he's doing.

"What's this calculation?" I ask.

He doesn't respond.

"Why are you all being so secretive?"

I want my question to sound like a joke, but my tone is earnest.

"That's how I told them to be." I hear Višnja's voice behind me.

"You don't trust me?" I ask.

I already know the answer. We worked together for years, after all.

"Not one bit," she says.

"You have no reason to doubt me. I've changed. I read books now."

Višnja laughs.

"The warming melted the Arctic, but it'll never thaw your face."

I act as if I haven't heard the insult. Višnja is right. My face looks the same even when I'm crying. Nothing can soften it. I look like a villain. I know that.

"Genetics are to blame," I say.

"Look at this," Vilko says to Gmaz.

He wants to stop the argument. When I turn my head, Višnja's no longer in the garage. I love invoking genetics because this is another part of Balkan heritage: genetics, money, and rakija. Whenever Višnja came home with me during our studies, she was repulsed by conversation with my parents. They always brought up the same subjects. When my father claimed I'd inherited my mother's looks and his brains, Višnja rolled her eyes. I never met her parents. I don't even know where she's from.

"Are you even from here?" I asked her once.

"It doesn't matter," she said.

But it did matter. That's why she hid it.

No one dares to install the console until Višnja returns. I offer to go over the software with Gmaz and review the elements they're unsure about, but they refuse me. I sit there for fifteen minutes in total silence. Even Vilko doesn't address me. Finally I get up and leave. Višnja isn't in the kitchen to say goodbye to.

On my way back home, I stop by the house of a neighbor who resells speedboats and motorboats. I write down the numbers I memorized from Gmaz's console on a piece of paper.

"This'll take a few days," my neighbor says, "but it shouldn't be a problem."

"Thanks," I say.

"Thank you," he replies.

The company he founded was doing well even before the flooding, and has since become indispensable. He's profited from others' misfortune. I'd invested a lot of money in him. It's paying off.

"Are you okay?" Vilko asks the next time he pays me a visit.

We haven't spoken all week.

"I've seen better days," I say.

My neighbor has procured the console. I didn't need to pay for it. There's never been a day better than today, but Vilko doesn't need to know that.

"You know Višnja," he says. "She holds grudges."

After I began to earn serious money from programming, Višnja asked me to donate to her work at the Institute. She wanted to devote herself more fully to theories that weren't lucrative. Ideas too abstract even for theoretical physics often ended up at the bottom of a drawer in the accounting department. Višnja didn't think in terms of the market, so she wasn't bringing in enough money for the Institute. I could have helped her, but I didn't want to.

"You must understand that I just didn't believe time travel was possible then," I tell Vilko.

"You don't have to explain," he says.

"Višnja will never let me go with you."

"She will, don't worry."

"She's suspicious. I don't know why."

"She thinks you're going to sabotage us."

"Don't be ridiculous," I say. "No one wants to get out of here more than I do."

"I know, but Višnja believes you don't actually want to help, and that you'll take a valuable spot we could instead give to a biologist or some other expert who'd warn the Yugoslav public about global warming."

"All I said to her was that I wasn't sure anyone in the Communist Party of Yugoslavia would entertain the ideas of time travel and global warming."

"We have to try," says Vilko.

"But why 1964 exactly, and why Yugoslavia? Why not the United States? A few years later? People didn't even have the internet then."

"The communists were the avant-garde. Yugoslavia was nonaligned. Višnja's afraid this could fall into the wrong hands. She wants to get to Kardelj and Krleža."

"Višnja's a fool!" I shout.

"There's nothing foolish about her intentions. Don't forget that the machine is partly Bakić's creation. He would be the first to recognize the polyvalent forms he explored and constructed in those years."

"She's looking for an artist to help her fight global warming? Don't make me laugh."

Višnja is by no means a fool. But I would never admit that. Everything Vilko's said makes sense, but I have different plans. Now that I've procured a steering console like the one they're planning to use for the trip, I can finally relax. I sleep better. I no longer have nightmares about drowning. I feel a euphoria I found before only in a bottle of sweet and syrupy cherry rakija.

"She only wants what's best for us," Vilko says.

"I'm not sure Višnja is the person who should be deciding what's best for me," I say. "I think there are people at the Institute who would make a different, more responsible decision."

Vilko gets up suddenly. He understands my threat.

"I told you you're coming with us. This is Višnja's life's work. You can't deny that."

"Tell her I want a place in the time machine. I want to get out of here."

"If you'd read Miroslav Krleža, you'd understand us better," Vilko says as he's leaving.

Night has already fallen when Višnja calls me.

"Okay, you can come with us," she says.

Blackmail always works. Even when I'm sober.

The first major floods began in 2014. The levees from the Yugoslav era hadn't been maintained, and people had illegally used backhoes to steal sand from the banks of the Sava River, destroying the shoreline and leaving their houses exposed. Italians had illegally hunted protected species of birds with rented guns and smuggled them across the border back to Italy. The clear-cutting of forests had intensified. Green spaces had been concreted over and the water had no place to flow. I remember it perfectly because Višnja would never stop talking about what would happen if people didn't change. She'd predicted the catastrophe. Experts around the world had agreed with her, but I'd just buried my father and couldn't have cared less. I don't want to make excuses, but the fact is that we can't always ponder big problems when private sorrows are plaguing us. My biggest problem was my mother, not global warming. A few years later, Višnja frantically read and recounted the UN's report on carbon dioxide emissions. She sent it to everyone on the Institute's mailing list. People began to look askance at her. They wanted to earn their wages and vacation on the Adriatic coast. They didn't care to think about the water rising to their front doors. Such an outcome sounded like science fiction.

"The Arctic is melting," Višnja told her colleagues. "We're going to lose Dalmatia and Istria. We're going to be left without a coast."

But what was an iceberg to me when I had a mother? I carried a flask with my favorite višnjevača to work every day. Theoretical physics wasn't helping, programming wasn't helping–I even grew numb to money. Vilko and Višnja took me out for dinner a few times, and paid the check even though I had much more money. They were good people, but that didn't help either. When I thought about Višnja's time machine, it seemed to me that no place existed in the space-time continuum that would get me far enough away from my problems. Maybe the point of singularity would help, I thought as I sipped on rakija. Either way, I didn't want to give Višnja money for her research.

If I'm understanding Vilko correctly on the phone, we need to set off on the trip to 1964 in three days. Our connection is poor and I have to call him back.

"The computer is causing interference," he says.

I hear noise in the background. Apparently Višnja is testing the console and the emergency brake.

"What should I bring?" I ask.

"Nothing but water," Vilko says.

Over the next three days I finish my own console and test its function with a remote control. The keys work and I practice using them. At the moment when Višnja types in the destination year, I'll quickly reenter her input. I'm not sure if it'll include any kind of authorization code. Actually, I am sure that it must because she still doesn't trust me, especially now that she's been confronted with my threats. To her mind the year 1964 means survival, but I don't trust people who don't lie. People who don't lie and scheme don't want to survive at all costs. Višnja has scruples, and as far as I'm concerned that's her biggest weakness. Survival demands the worst of us. Of course I'm careful not to let Vilko detect that I'm planning something–he'd immediately inform Višnja and the rest of the crew. They still believe science should be noble.

While I'm working on the console I have no time to read, though Vilko's allusion to Krleža has intrigued me. It's too late to find one of his books. Višnja values only that progress which has no relationship to money, so I assume that this author, this Miroslav Krleža, shares her values. I'm not familiar with the other communist Vilko mentioned. Kardelj something, but to me it's not important.

I disassemble the console and put the most important part into a much smaller casing I can easily hide in my sleeve. I have a copy of the program Višnja wrote for the time machine on my computer. It isn't hard to modify the design. Despite our troubles with flooding, technology has continued to advance.

"You can come now," Vilko says on the phone three days later.

Before I climb into my boat, I look around. I want to remember the future I'm about to irreversibly abandon. Instead of water, I bring the console and a favorite photograph of me and my parents standing in the orchard. To my father's left is the blooming cherry, our favorite family tree.

When I arrive at the garage, everyone is ready and bursting from excitement. They can't do a test run because they're not certain they can return to the exact same moment they've departed from. The time machine isn't totally reliable in that way, but Višnja claims that the journey through a wormhole in one direction is as real as the reality of global warming. Everyone has absolute faith in her. She knows what she's doing.

"We have only one chance," she says. "Every trip after that will vary randomly by plus or minus 300 years. Maybe even more. The coordinates I've inputted are a safety net, but they're no guarantee."

I close my eyes for a moment and imagine space bending at the time machine's command.

"Are you ready?" Višnja asks me.

"Yes," I lie.

Fink and Gmaz sit as Vilko described, at the back of the machine. A piece of Bakić juts out above their heads. Višnja takes her seat at the steering console. Vilko sits on her right, and I on her left. I have my back turned to her.

"Testing, one, two, three," she says in a loud voice.

I hear buttons being pressed and the safety switch being activated. I assume she's unlocked the time machine with her thumbprint. Then, on my own miniature console, which I've synchronized with hers, I see that Višnja has typed in March 1, 1964. Vilko explains that it's important for us to arrive at a point in that year prior to the convening of the Eighth Congress of the League of Communists of Yugoslavia in Belgrade. There the Yugoslav communists will repeal the *Five-Year Plan: 1961-1965* and announce the "great economic reform" that will open up Yugoslav society to a market economy and capitalism.

"Our problems began in December 1964," he says. "We need to show Edvard Kardelj the consequences. He needs to see them."

He's referring to the high rate of unemployment that followed, but not just that, because in Višnja's brilliant mind everything is connected: the free market, economic inequality, inflation, and global warming. Vilko's just repeating her meaningful words, emulating her brilliance. She's always seen the big picture. The picture in the forefront of my mind is my family photograph. We sit huddled together in the time machine, but there are light years between us. It's impossible to reconcile our ideologies. Vilko's been a fool to try to keep us together. He's been a fool to trust me.

Right before Višnja starts the machine, I input the year 1740 on my console. The change doesn't show quickly enough on her monitor to be noticed. She presses the button that's supposed to take us to Zagreb in 1964.

Gmaz is the first to disembark. He vomits, of course, because the machine has wrung us out like wet beach towels. Before he can look up, out jumps Fink, who's tolerated the time travel much better.

"This isn't Zagreb," he says.

He points to Versailles.

"What is that?" says Višnja, dumbfounded.

"Versailles."

"What year?" she asks. "How did we end up here?"

She looks at me. Then she looks at my hands. She sees the reserve console.

"Idiot!" she screams. "What have you done?"

"I've returned us to better days. Isn't that what you wanted?"

"What year is this?" Fink asks.

"It's 1740," I say.

Vilko is silent. I know he's consumed by the sweet feeling of guilt.

"This is awful," he eventually says. "None of us knows French."

"You're wrong," I say cheerfully.

Unlike them, I speak the language fluently.

"I can teach you how to say *višnja* in French—it's *cerise*," I say. "Learn that word well because you're going to need it."

Everyone is visibly upset. They don't even know where to start with eighteenth-century France, but I'm more than ready. We have about fifty years until the revolution, in which Višnja will surely fare well. But now we're on my turf: we've come to the most delightful, most debauched age of Louis XV. I'm looking forward to the outrageous behavior of his courtiers.

"We're in for some sweet cherry-picking," I say.

The eighteenth century promises different rhythms, devoid of consequences I might personally face. Višnja is crying. Seeing her tears, I feel an onrush of positive emotions I haven't known in a long time, not since my mother's death.

TO EVERYTHING, TERN TERN TERN
by Birna Anna Björnsdóttir

MY MOTHER DISAPPEARED ON JUNE 1, 2040, which happened to be my twenty-first birthday. She'd seemed in fine spirits a few days earlier when she left, with a group of students from the high school where she taught biology, for a study trip to the Faroe Islands, a trip she had taken a number of times before. The day after she went missing, I was contacted by her fellow teacher on the tour. He told me that on the previous day the two of them had taken the twenty or so students on one of the longer hikes on their itinerary, up to some of the more remote cliffs on the main island, where they had been able to observe seabirds such as fulmars, guillemots, and puffins hunting and tending to their young. It was a damp and foggy day but they had made some pretty impressive sightings and returned to their hostel in downtown Thorshofn feeling satisfyingly fatigued. After dinner the two teachers retired to bed and when her colleague knocked on my mother's door the following morning she didn't answer. He checked the breakfast hall and lobby area, and then asked the receptionist for a key to her room. When he opened the door he found it empty, save for a single piece of paper left on a table by the window. On it she had jotted notes about local birds, along with numbers and some clinical observations.

On June 9, I sat on a rock by the sea in my hometown of Seltjarnarnes, a neighboring town to Reykjavík, holding the note between my fingers. I wore fingerless mittens so I could touch the paper she had touched and trace the letters she had written for the gazillionth time. I'd been going to that same spot every day since I'd learned of my mother's disappearance, to this area that used to be a golf course but was now too cold and windy for even the heartiest of my compatriots to tough it out. This had once been a fine place for golf during the summer season, one that was still very much in use the year I was born, but a few years ago people gave up trying. Right next to the golf course there had been an expansive nesting ground for the Arctic tern–*kría* in Icelandic. My mother named me after that bird, her favorite. "No bird, pardon me, no *creature*, comes close to the kría, the most fascinating animal on the planet! The strongest, most precise, most determined, most graceful, and with grit and stamina rivaled by nothing!" This, or some version of this, she would declare regularly with dramatic flair, and it felt good, as a kid, to be named after such a magnificent beast. Not a lot of people in Iceland had traditionally been given the name Kría. I'm one of only a handful of people with it my age and older, although it became increasingly popular after the kría stopped nesting here. When changes in the acidity of the ocean around Iceland decimated the population of the sand eel, the tern's main source of sustenance, the bird was forced to shift its migration pattern, bypassing Iceland. Losing our beloved tern, a bird at once adored and taken for granted as part of what we knew as the landscape of home, seemed to bring on a wave of wistful, nostalgic namings of Icelandic baby girls, and sitting there then it stung to think about the pathetic human inability to properly celebrate what you have while you have it. I removed the note from my pocket once more, stroking it, gazing at my mother's familiar handwriting, mining the piece of paper for clues I knew were not there.

My mother–*mamma* in Icelandic–had me at an "advanced maternal age," I believe is the technical term. She was forty-four, and although her unexpected pregnancy was big news to anyone who knew her at the time, nobody was more surprised than she. Mamma had dedicated her life to science. She never made it through a PhD but had a basic degree in biology, and, after studying nature on her own throughout her life, eventually came to teach it. She had the introverted and slightly freewheeling personality of an autodidact. I think she was a bit too much of a rebel to work within the formal structure of the academic system, or, like many people of her generation, she might have been dealing with undiagnosed ADHD issues. I never really figured out which it was.

She didn't do well with relationships. I know she had a few boyfriends before I was born but I never knew of anyone after I came along. This is what I've been told: my father was a save-the-whales American who came to Iceland in the fall of 2018. He was trying to gather some steam for the whaling movement, but, as Mamma put it, he was a bit outdated in his subject matter–stagnated, really–and therefore not very effective. She said that all the successful and dynamic efforts of that time had a holistic outlook, taking into consideration the climate crisis as a whole and the unprecedented existential crisis threatening *all* species, while he was fixated only on the plight of the whales. But, he was devastatingly attractive and after a long night at a downtown bar arguing over the merits of tunnel vision versus an all-encompassing approach to environmentalism they had a brief fling. He left the country before she had a chance to tell him she was pregnant. She decided to leave it that way.

Mamma hadn't thought it was possible to become a mother at her age. She had never been especially keen on having children, but after thinking long and hard about the environmental ethics of bringing another human being into the world, and factoring in the small miracle of becoming pregnant at this stage in her life, she decided to have me. I was born on June 1, 2019, and by then Mamma had moved in with my grandmother so that she could help her care for me in my infancy. Twenty-one years later we still lived there.

When my grandmother–*amma*–and I tried to make sense of Mamma's disappearance, Amma remained her characteristically stoic self, reminding me how a rash, anxiety-driven restlessness had always been an integral part of Mamma's personality and how she had learned, mostly, to manage these impulses so as to live a relatively unruffled life on the surface.

"It's the climate," I said, sobbing. "This climate stuff, it's finally managed to push her over the edge." Mamma had become an environmental activist in Iceland in the '90s, long before it became mainstream. Around the time I was born people's fears about the climate crisis had started to become pretty acute, and by then my mother had gotten practically militant. All of this seemed to have a progressively negative effect on her mental health as she became more and more consumed with impending disaster and simple everyday functions became increasingly fraught with doom. To her, things like the occasional non-vegan hot dog, an item of fast fashion, or a disposable bag that couldn't be avoided on a spontaneous trip to the grocery store all marked the beginning of a slippery slope toward the planet's ultimate downfall. When I'd share my concerns about her state of mind with Amma, she would tell me that Mamma had always had these tendencies. The climate crisis and the colossal-scale damage we'd seen to the environment in my lifetime, the melting of the ice caps making coastal areas in many places of the world largely uninhabitable, changes in the oceans' acidity levels disrupting the ecosystems within and around them, the extinction of countless species of flora and fauna—all of this had, in my grandmother's opinion, been an expedient vehicle for my mother's innate tendencies to worry and catastrophize.

As a child in the '80s, Mamma had agonized over what she thought was an impending nuclear annihilation. She was certain that a Soviet submarine spying on the U.S. naval base in Keflavik would either bomb the base, leaving us as collateral damage, or accidentally spill some of its nuclear materials in our oceans, giving us all cancer. After the Chernobyl disaster, Mamma didn't get out of bed for a week. It seemed to confirm her wildest and most painful fears and she was certain that the same fate would meet us all, but on a more formidable scale. When Reagan and Gorbachev managed to make nice, here in Iceland of all places, Amma was thrilled. The de-escalation of the power play between Moscow and Washington was great, of course, but more importantly her anxious little girl would now have a chance to regain her equilibrium. Amma even took an eleven-year-old Mamma down to Hofdi, the leaders' meeting place in Reykjavík, and stood with her at the side of the road to see the motorcades so that she could point and say, *Look, these guys are going to make a deal to not bomb each other or any of us folks.* What a great lesson for a little girl, I thought grimly in my current state of worry, to learn how two big men could be such bosses of the world.

Throughout her adolescence and young adulthood, Mamma always remained moderately tense about one thing or another, but it wasn't until the climate crisis came along that her mind found something to grab onto with the same vigor as it had the Cold War.

"She was always afraid of *something*," Amma explained. "For years it was nuclear winter. That never happened. *Then* it was the climate crisis."

"But Amma, that *did* happen."

"That's not the point, sweetie."

In Amma's view, Mamma had something broken inside her all along; her concern for the environment was secondary. All the changes and tragedies the world had seen in the past few years were secondary. I didn't buy that. To me things were much more intertwined. They had to be.

The ruins of the golf course and nesting grounds seemed even more desolate than usual as I stood up and surveyed them before heading home. The sea levels around here had risen almost a meter in my lifetime, making this area that used to be solid dry ground now wet and swampy. Everything happened much faster than they had projected: half a meter in thirty years became a meter in only twenty. But this was the least of our problems. As I marched through the damp straw in my hiking boots, the mushy underlay made sounds that took me back to my early childhood, when I'd join Mamma on–in the jargon of that era–self-care retreats in the highlands of Iceland. They would set up sweat lodges, bring over some shamans, and drink psychedelic cocoa under the guise of some ambiguous spirituality. With the current state of things, such frivolity could no longer be afforded. But, characteristically, Mamma had been into all that stuff for a while. She was always searching; I see that now. I am much more like Amma. Or maybe my father, who knows.

On my way back to the main road, the limp yellow-grayish straws covered the marshy terrain as successfully as a bad toupee. This unsightliness was crowned by the enormous house on the edge of what used to be the golf course. It couldn't have been more appropriately awful-looking, a cold concrete box with the only windows facing the sea, its grotesque largeness an embodiment of all it stood for.

The house belonged to a man named Arthur, a hedge-fund manager from New York who had made a small fortune betting on what would happen to us here in Iceland as a result of the climate crisis. Around the time I was born the accepted prediction said we would get a more pleasant climate. We were looped into what was thought of as the likeliest scenario for most of the Arctic region, that the most influential change to our day-to-day living conditions would be higher temperatures. People envisioned balmier summers and milder winters, coupled with profound changes in our icescapes, of course, causing a rise in sea levels that would encroach upon coastal areas. The higher temperatures were also supposed to cause changes in our flora and fauna, forcing some species to go elsewhere or to become extinct and introducing new ones to our region. The most dreaded of these would be pesky insects, the comforting refrain during eternally awful Icelandic weather having always been *at least we don't have mosquitoes*.

This predicted warming did happen in most Arctic communities. Many of them had completely transformed—namely Greenland, which was now booming with new and growing towns on land that emerged from underneath glaciers in coastal areas high enough to remain above water. Greenland's landmass, most of which had always been covered with ice, was large enough for multiple extremely livable areas to develop along its coastline. With its brand-new economic pillars—servicing the shipping routes between East Asia and North America made possible by the shrinking of the polar ice caps, and the influx of climate immigrants who gave up on the unbearable summer heats of mainland Europe—and its newly pleasant climate and living conditions, Greenland was on its way to becoming one of Europe's most prosperous and desirable countries.

What happened here in Iceland, on the other hand, was something scientists had thought of as only a minor possibility, and this guy Arthur had found a way of tying this into a complicated financial instrument and placing a large bet on it. With the melting of the ice caps and rerouting of ocean currents, the Gulf Stream—an ocean current Iceland had forever relied on for its relatively temperate climate—had changed its course so that it now bypassed the country. This change had begun around ten years ago, and had since made Iceland's climate vastly colder and harsher. What used to be an annoyingly cold and stormy but bearable winter was now a season where people went for days and sometimes weeks without leaving their houses. They stocked supplies, worked from home, and semi-homeschooled their kids, effectively hibernating for long stretches during the winter months–and these were people who for decades, for centuries, had claimed that there was no such thing as bad weather, only bad clothes. The summers now brought us what before would have been considered mild winter weather, and the big question looming was whether Iceland was, in fact, still habitable. A lot of people had left already, many to Greenland (oh, the irony that the names of our two countries finally made sense) and some to the Scandinavian countries. Those countries had plenty of problems of their own to deal with, by the way, with even *their* summers now becoming unbearably hot, and their space and resources running low from vast immigration from the south and now also the north.

Arthur had placed this enormous bet on the rerouting of the Gulf Stream a few decades back by creating a set of complicated bonds. And when this became our reality in the '30s he made an obscene amount of money. To give back, as he put it, he decided to build a vacation home in Iceland, and also to dedicate a sum each year to supporting life- and earth-science education in local communities. He struck a deal with the town of Seltjarnarnes, which sold him this particular lot to build his house (the golf course was closing down anyway), and in return he committed to funding research and educational projects within the town. The annual trip Mamma took with her students to observe birds in the Faroe Islands was one of them.

As I approached the main road I heard the door of the house opening. I turned around and saw a guy my age walking out, presumably Arthur's son–Arthur Jr., go figure. He saw me and jogged my way. I was in no mood to talk to a stranger so I pulled the hood on my jacket even tighter around my head as I marched on.

"Wait," he called after me. Figuring there was no way out of this, I stopped. As I turned around he flashed a smile that was either confident or rehearsed, it was hard to tell, and reached out his right hand.

"Hi, I'm Arthur."

"I'm Kría," I said without smiling back.

"Oh, I know who you are." My quizzical expression encouraged him to keep talking.

"You're that girl, the daughter of that teacher who went missing. I've seen you sitting out here these past few days. I can only imagine what you must be going through."

He seemed earnest enough in his concern. I didn't quite know what to make of him, having never met the guy. I'd only heard that the owner of the house had a son my age. People in town had a mild interest in gossiping about these fellows but there didn't seem to be much information on them beyond their matching names.

"Thanks," I said, turning back toward home. I'd been so low-energy these past few days that just leaving the house to sit by the ocean was a huge effort, let alone partaking in conversation with anyone besides Amma. I started walking again and he gently took a few steps alongside me.

"I'd like to help you."

The frigid June air had started to blow forcefully. I tried telling him that I had to get home, but he insisted on walking with me. I didn't have the strength to argue. On the way he told me that he and his father felt partially responsible for what had happened to my mother, seeing as they had funded the trip, and that he would like to help me find her. I told him that was absurd, they bore no responsibility, the trip had gone the way it had gone, it didn't matter who had funded it. But he insisted.

"She wouldn't have been in the Faroes that day if it weren't for us." At this I couldn't help myself.

"Calm down boy, you're not *that* important."

He laughed. "You're funny," he said.

Why do guys always say that? I thought.

On the walk I learned that he had just graduated from college in the U.S. and that his mission in life now was to make this fragile and suffering world a better place, his words. He didn't need to work, again his words, and wanted to use his privilege (and ease his rich-kid conscience, my words) to help those in need. His long-term plan was to give away most of his wealth to benevolent organizations and charities and, of course, start up his own charitable fund, focusing on the environment and especially the Arctic areas, as they and their predicament happened to be the source of his family's wealth.

"Why don't you donate to an organization that works to dismantle the system that allows people like you to make and keep such a disproportionate amount of wealth in the first place?"

We stopped in front of my house, the house in which both Mamma and I had grown up. I saw Amma through the kitchen window, preparing our dinner of breaded fried cod and potatoes. He paused and for a moment I thought he was going to tell me I was funny again, but instead he said, "Wow. What a powerful idea." As soon as he said this, he seemed to regret it, and, looking slightly embarrassed, he added: "I know, I have a lot to learn, I'm really trying. I'm trying to be different than, well, you know, trying to do things differently."

Before he left he asked me to think about letting him take me to the Faroe Islands in his jet ("It runs on biofuels only, don't worry") so that I could take a look around, talk to some people, see if there might be any clues to my mother's disappearance. I told him I would think about it. He hesitated before walking off and then turned again and said, "I can't pretend to understand your situation, but still, I know a little bit what it's like to feel like they've just checked out on you."

When Amma spotted us through the kitchen window and gestured for me to invite this new friend in for fish and potatoes, I immediately sent him on his way and dashed inside. Underneath Arthur Jr.'s insistence on helping me, it seemed there had to be a story about his own parents. I took a peek through the small glass window in the front door and watched him wrap his unzipped jacket tightly around himself as he walked away. Before stepping into the kitchen, I dialed Mamma's number for what had to be the hundredth time since her disappearance. Like all those other times, it went straight to voicemail.

The following afternoon, on June 10, I gave Amma a tight and tearful hug as she told me to stay strong and ushered me along the tarmac at Reykjavík Airport toward the ten-seat jet decorated in shimmering white and icy blue, ARCTIC DREAM PURVEYOR written on it in a whimsical font. Arthur Jr. was standing by the mobile stairway leading up to the door of the jet, his smile from the day before intact. He greeted me cheerfully, though with appropriately somber undertones, as if to underscore his awareness that this trip was obviously not going to be easy for me.

"Does it run on olive oil?" I asked to keep the mood light as we walked up the stairs. He laughed. "No, canola."

Gazing out the window as we took off, I saw Reykjavík and Seltjarnarnes receding in my view, the pond in the city center slowly becoming a coin and then a dot. Junior had considerately taken a seat a few rows behind me and was quaintly engaged in a book. I, on the other hand, was happy to doze off, given my unprecedented tiredness these past few days. As my thoughts started floating I recalled what my mother had taught me about my bird, her bird, the Arctic tern. I was so tiny when she first told me about the tern that I don't remember ever not knowing about its unbelievable nature, and throughout my childhood and adolescence she would regularly recount its way of life to me, always with the same delight as if she were telling me all of it for the first time. Each year the tern migrates effectively from the South Pole to the North Pole and back. After spending the winter in Antarctica she sets out for her nesting grounds in the north, where she spends the summer, and then flies south again for winter. But our winter is of course summer in Antarctica, so the tern basically spends her life in perpetual summer. And with polar summers' twenty-four hours of daylight, it's only during her flights back and forth that she ever sees the dark. She always finds her way, she always finds her same nesting spot. She spends around sixty days on her journey north, soaring and gliding along with advantageous wind currents. It's even said that she takes brief naps while flying (in Iceland we call a power nap a kría). The same journey south takes around ninety days. On that route the terns fly around the southern tip of Africa; birds leaning into beneficial wind flow have been tracked going all the way over to Australia and back en route to their feeding grounds in Antarctica. No other creature undertakes such a long annual migration journey. The Arctic tern weighs around one hundred eighty grams, less than half a pound, less than a small can of soda. A tern usually lives into her twenties with some becoming as old as thirty. By then, having flown anywhere from thirty to forty thousand miles a year, depending on where up north she nests, a tern will have flown a distance equivalent to flying to the moon and back three times.

I stirred as the jet touched down at Thorshofn airport. Despite all of Mamma's trips to the Faroes and her fascination with the place, I'd never been there before.

Upon disembarking I realized that I didn't have much of a plan. I'd just thought we'd check into the same hostel Mamma had stayed at and take it from there. Arthur Jr. clearly had other ideas. It turned out that he had rented a house not too far from the airport, something of a palace by Faroese standards. As the car dropped him off there, I insisted upon going downtown.

"I'm good at the hostel," I told him. "I need to be there."

"Of course. I understand," he said with appropriate solemnity. I promised to call him if I needed literally anything, as he put it. On the way downtown I called Mamma's number, which went directly to voicemail. I called again. And then again.

At the hostel, I asked the receptionist if I could have the same room my mother had had. They immediately knew who I was and warmly accommodated me. Entering the room felt stranger than I was prepared for. She had been here a little over a week ago. She had slept on this bed. She had had all of her things here. Made decisions here. Or had she made them long before? I didn't feel her presence, though, which, as someone who sort of believes in ghosts, I took as a good sign.

I started rummaging through drawers, cabinets, and wastebaskets. I even looked under the bedsheets. I found nothing. I went down to the lobby in the hopes of meeting more of the hotel staff. I was told that my mother had left nothing in her room besides that piece of paper with the bird notes, that nobody had seen her leave the hotel the night she disappeared. I was also told to keep in mind that no one had been manning the reception between midnight and 5:30 a.m.

I went upstairs to fetch my coat and headed out for a walk. During my aimless stroll through the city center that with all its newness bore an uncanny resemblance to home, I sifted through some of Mamma's peculiarities. I remembered her quite frequently going away on her own on the weekends when I was a kid, on trips to the countryside, or abroad (she'd carbon-neutralize all of her flights, of course), and if that wasn't possible she'd retreat to her room with the door closed for entire Sundays. I didn't make much of it at the time, it was just my normal, but when I was a teenager I sometimes wondered whether Mamma might actually want to be someplace other than where she was. Stuck with me and Amma. I didn't think too much about her possible fragility; frankly, I didn't understand it. It just bothered me that she couldn't be more normal, that she couldn't be more like Amma.

The Arctic tern is what is referred to in biology as a K-selected breeder, a creature that spends considerable time raising relatively few offspring. The tern is an aggressive nester and a fierce defender of her young. When threatened she will attack humans and other large predators by striking them on the top of their head with her beak, and although she is too small to cause serious injury, she is capable of drawing blood and thus repelling her potential predators, which range from smaller mammals to polar bears.

The following morning I woke up early and called Arthur to ask if he could arrange a car to take me up to the nesting grounds where Mamma had gone with her students the day before she went missing. Arthur offered to come along, but I told him I'd rather go by myself. As I walked from the breakfast hall through the reception area toward the front door to check for the car, the receptionist told me that a letter had just arrived. I looked at the envelope and my heart stopped. I read my name above the hotel's address in my mother's handwriting. The postage stamp was dated June 4. I double- and triple-checked the date before noticing the postmark: SOUTH AFRICA.

I urgently tore open the envelope only to find another envelope inside it. It said: READ THIS WHEN YOU GET TO THE CLIFFS. I put both envelopes carefully in my coat pocket, zipped it closed, and walked straight to the car waiting for me outside. As I sat in the backseat and we drove through narrow, windy roads, my heart racing in step with my thoughts, I didn't feel all that surprised. I had known she had to be somewhere. Just as she had known I would be here.

The driver stopped at the end of a gravel road and told me to follow the small river up into the valley and turn off to the right when the land began to steepen. From there I would get access to some of the lower sea cliffs, he said, and definitely see some puffins and guillemots. He told me he'd be waiting for me in the same spot. I started walking and made my way through the wet lowland area for a while, looking out for changes in the landscape, which remained flat and didn't appear to heighten within my range of sight. And then suddenly I heard them, their warning sounds preceding my sightings. Though I hadn't seen or heard any terns since they left Iceland, I recognized them immediately: the gray and white bodies and heads capped with black, their distinct sounds yanking me back to the '20s, when I was a small child in Seltjarnarnes and spent what seemed like hours on end gazing at these birds and their swift, balletic movements. I remembered an old trick Mamma had taught me when walking through their nesting grounds: find a stick and hold it high over your head, as the terns always go for the highest spot. On the ground in front of me was a stick that looked like it had broken off of a larger piece of driftwood; the shape was a little awkward but it would do. I held it up high and trod carefully, my eyes glued to the ground so I wouldn't accidentally step on any of the precious eggs. The terns' cries intensified above me as I marched through their territory. I held the stick firmly in my hand, feeling a sharp tap or two on its tip as I neared what appeared to be the center of the birds' domain. I tried to spot the shortest way out of this vast nesting area, to somewhere I could find the path to the cliffs, but it wasn't obvious, and in my depleted state I was wary of a long and strenuous hike. I was tempted to just take a seat where I was. As desperate as I was to read the letter, she had told me to read it at the cliffs and it was in my nature to be obedient. I always followed instructions immaculately, especially from Mamma and Amma. But as I strode there wielding my stick, watching my step, aggressively deliberate, an unfamiliar feeling crept up on me. I was in charge.

I sat down on a mound with dry straws on the surface and soft soil underneath. I kept the stick up high with one arm, the terns circling above my head, their cries approaching screams. I unzipped my pocket with my other hand, took out the envelope, and managed to open it with my teeth. It held a one-page handwritten letter from Mamma.

Dearest Kría,

I don't have to tell you much, most of the things I could tell you you already know. You are twenty-one now. My job is done and I have space now to go and figure some things out, to see if I can fix myself a bit. How middle-aged of me, but you know that clichés are clichés for a reason. I ask you to forgive me. I had to do it this way, to go off the grid for a while. I need this time and I ask you in the strongest possible way not to worry about me. I may be delicate but I am not weak. Know that you are loved, you always were, and you always will be. I know it's a lot to ask a daughter to show her flawed mother this type of understanding, but I also know that you are mature beyond your years. You had to be.

As you might have noticed from the postmark, I'm writing this from South Africa. And as you've likely figured out as well, being as intelligent as you are, my darling, I have set out to trace and follow the migration pattern of my bird, your bird, our kría.

I don't know how long or far this will take me. Please fulfill your own dreams and know that you could do nothing better for me.

To everything there is a season, my sweet Kría. A time to build up, a time to break down, a time to dance, a time to mourn, a time to plant, a time to reap.

Listen to that song every now and then.

Your mamma

I was so lost in reading and rereading the letter that I had unwittingly lowered my stick to the ground. I was forcefully jerked back to the present by a sharp pain on the top of my head. I wasn't wearing a hat so the bird had full access to my scalp, which I realized it had managed to pierce when I touched my head and took it away to see a decent amount of blood in the palm of my hand. I instantly grabbed the stick and raised it again, tucking the letter into my pocket and zipping it up before making my way back to the car.

Over the next few weeks and months, the obnoxious yap of a common seagull, a non-vegan hamburger, driving past Hofdi in Reykjavík, a disposable candy wrapper–every minor detail of daily life led me back to Mamma and the burden of these unresolved circumstances. Everyone told me that time would heal me, make me feel better, but the more time passed the worse I seemed to feel. As much as I had at times taken Mamma for granted, dismissed her, relied first and foremost on Amma throughout my life, her absence left a void in me larger than her presence had ever felt. Having been cut loose in this way, I was left obsessive in my quest to become whole again. I knew I had to find a way to regain my sense of place in the world, or at least to readjust it.

On October 1, I went back to the Faroe Islands. I flew with Arthur Jr. in his jet from Reykjavík to Thorshofn again. Before we left for the Faroes I told him that from there I'd set off to go looking for Mamma. My plan was to take a boat to Denmark, make my way down through Europe and then West Africa, following the tern's migration path as closely as possible. From South Africa I would go to Australia and from there to New Zealand, where I would take an excursion by sea to Antarctica.

I said goodbye to Arthur Jr. at the harbor and boarded the ship to Denmark. I made my way to the upper deck and took in the open sea as I inserted my earphones and turned on that seventy-five-year-old song by the Byrds that Mamma had referenced in her letter. Breathing in the cold salty air, I felt lighter than I had in months. A sense of knowing I was on the right path came over me with new certainty. Amma had been supportive of my plan, not because she thought I'd find her, I'm sure, but because she recognized how determined I was to try.

A time to cast away stones, a time to gather stones together.

I didn't know if I'd ever get her back. But I knew there were many ways for me to find her, or at least to reclaim parts of her. When the ship set out to sea and Thorshofn harbor got smaller and smaller, the sparkling waves crashing onto the boat's keel, I noticed a small group of terns finding their groove in the wake of the ship, feeling out the gales conjured up by its speed, gauging whether these air currents might be of any use to them. And then, as one, the terns seemed to decide that these would not do, and they took to the higher skies in a sweeping, synchronized motion.

SAVE YOURSELF
by Abbey Mei Otis

THE PHONE RINGS AND AMALIA has a premonition: *Don't answer it*. She can't imagine where the whisper comes from, and she resents it. The idea of being ruled by anything beyond her understanding is intolerable. She jabs the green button.

"Oh my god. *Darcy!*"

The last time she saw Darcy, they were both eighteen. The past ten years have stripped the baby fat from Darcy's face. Her features look more solid, though Amalia wonders if this is just the difference between distant memory and the reality of a phone screen. She hopes it is authentic, hopes she also presents a more substantial version of herself.

Darcy looks nervous. "I'm in the area for work. I know it's been a while, but–"

"Oh my god, no, it's wonderful. You have to come by. You have to." Sitting on the gray sectional in the sunroom, Amalia angles the phone so the blown-glass vase in its alcove is framed over her shoulder. "Please. I'm dying of boredom out here."

"Okay." Darcy rotates her septum ring with a knuckle. The gesture is so thoroughly her that Amalia nearly tears up. "I don't want to intrude." Behind Darcy's head, Amalia can see a car's rear window framing a landscape speeding past.

"Shut up. Are you in a car? Are you on your way right now?"

"Oh, we've been traveling for a long time." As Darcy says this, a great tiredness is suddenly apparent in her face, though her expression remains unchanged. Amalia worries for a moment that her own face looks the same kind of tired. She pans the phone so the camera takes in the picture window, the tree line, the clear sky beyond. She thinks, and then forgets to ask, *We?*

Amalia hears the car before she can see it. She is very attuned to sounds these days. She walks out on the front patio with ice cubes knocking in her tumbler. The car kicks up a cloud of dust as it approaches, wending its way down the narrow gravel road between two immense soy fields. Former soy fields. Amalia still names the land according to what once grew there, though Erik often tells her to stop.

Now the fields are fallow and empty, unfertilized, bare of moisture and minerals and nutrients and anything that might let something grow. Erik's family, and thus Amalia's family, holds as its kingdom forty thousand acres of dead baked earth. Darcy's car rolls up its windows as the dust cloud grows bigger. Amalia imagines how she must look, grandiose house surrounded by acres and acres of dirt. Dirt kingdom for a dirt queen.

The car pulls through the semicircle driveway and Darcy gets out on the passenger side. The back door rises, and a second, smaller figure emerges. Darcy leans through the window to tap something on the car's steering mechanism, and it rumbles away back down the long road.

Darcy's face on the phone looked aged, but in person her figure remains limber, boyish. She rakes a hand through short hair as she straightens up from the car. "Uh. Hi."

"Welcome!" Amalia hopes her enthusiasm covers her alarm at the smaller figure. Darcy can't have had a child. Could Darcy have had a child? She tries to calculate in her head. She has been imagining her own life as solid and adult, impressively so. She has been excited to share this new version of herself with Darcy. Okay, maybe more than excited, maybe a little proud, a little triumphant. And now the possibility that Darcy has leapfrogged her—how can Amalia's built-in bookshelves and smart-home sensors compete with motherhood?

Darcy comes in for a hug, whispers into her ear, "Hope it's cool, I'm watching the kid for a friend."

"Of course!" Amalia laughs. "Absolutely!"

The child leans into Darcy's hip as the two women hug. Darcy's clothes smell vaguely mildewed. Mollified, Amalia settles back into her role as benevolent host. "Oh my god, has it really been ten years?"

Darcy's brow knits and she nods. "Ten years."

Ten years ago they hadn't felt like children, but now, looking back, it is clear that they were.

The dust raised by the car begins to settle. You cannot set foot in this landscape for a minute before it claims you. Amalia washes her hair every morning, and every evening her scalp is grained with sand. Darcy watches the car vanish without any visible emotion, then turns to the child. "Can I introduce you?" The child gives no reaction that Amalia can perceive, but Darcy must see an affirmative, because she kneels and eases the child forward. "This is Vine."

Amalia would not say that she dislikes children, but she would say they always make her profoundly, helplessly awkward, and she dislikes that feeling. She bends at the waist instead of the knee so she looms over Vine. "Well, hi there!"

Vine smells of something antiseptic and unchildlike. Amalia straightens, tries not to sneeze. The child stares up at her with round, calculating eyes. Amalia has no idea how to estimate the age of a child—could they be nine? Twelve? Six?

Vine drops their eyes and seems to stare at nothing. Their shoulders wiggle uncertainly but the rest of their body is held stiff.

"Don't mind them." Darcy rubs Vine's shoulder. "They're not feeling great. They really pulled it together today."

"No, no, I'm glad they're here. It gets so adult around here, you know? And plus, we can show them the—" Long pause. What could she show a child? The recessed lighting? The wine cellar? "We can show them the new VR room!"

Vine perks up instantly. "Games?"

Darcy squeezes Vine's hand. "Be careful with those. Don't bump anything."

"Oh, it's fine, everything's padded," Amalia says.

Darcy shakes her head. "It's not that. They just need to be careful."

Vine slips free of Darcy's hand and skips toward the front door, calling over their shoulder, "Hurry up!"

"Vine, remember, we talked about politeness?"

Vine is hopping at the front door but Darcy pauses, watching Amalia. She rakes a hand through her hair again. "Sorry. It's weird, seeing you without your sister."

"I know." Amalia nods. "It would make her happy, don't you think?"

Darcy looks like she hadn't considered this. "Maybe. Yeah." She glances at the sky.

Ten years ago Amalia, her older sister Ayleen, and their parents were washed-out refugees from the Carolina coast. Their father shelled out his last paycheck to a relocation company that hauled them across Appalachia in a bus without AC, then dumped them in southern Ohio. The shelter they ended up in was also a processing center, vetting candidates for an upcoming Mars expedition. This one would study diet and body-mass retention techniques that could be sold to private colonists. The four of them had little flesh cores pinched out of their upper arms, then they were given a cubicle with four cots, partitioned off with curtains.

Ayleen raged at their parents, swore the minute she turned eighteen she would be gone from this shithole and their shitty decisions. Amalia withdrew into herself, pushed food around on her plate. Their father had always been full of new dreams, leaping from one idea to the next and leaving a trail of unfinished projects in his wake. He would enthusiastically pull the rest of them along with him, but the light in his eyes dimmed whenever they grew bored or asked a question he didn't like. His daughters came to realize they were useful to him only as an audience. Their mother clenched her mouth perpetually in a grim line. Always making hard choices with no happy option. Always, it seemed, oriented toward her children with fury buried just under the surface. Only a few times did her resentment break enough for gentleness to show through.

The sisters stayed so close that people often guessed they were twins, and then asked in a whisper what was wrong with Amalia. She was a fragile facsimile of her older sister. Identical dark curls, but Ayleen's were lustrous while Amalia's were flat. Olive skin, but Ayleen was tanned and golden while Amalia was ashy and inflamed. Same dark eyes, but Ayleen's were bright and deep while Amalia's were reddened and watery. Ayleen soldiered through the endless moves, the dry-rotted shelters, the synthetic food, with a hardiness that hinted at a lack of imagination, but Amalia developed asthma, endless allergies, so many food intolerances that her carefulness verged on compulsion. She could not eat the GMO wheat or corn or soy, no red meat or dairy if there had been red meat or dairy, no nuts, no alliums, no food that had sat out in the air, no food that had touched another food, no food that had to be picked up with her hands. Amalia, if you held her up to the sun, the light would show through.

In the daytime, when they had finished their rounds of repetitive tasks to measure muscle tone, the sisters wandered the facility. Darcy was the only other teenager there, a wild-eyed delinquent in the corner bunk, with heavy eyeliner and a more ostentatious version of her current septum ring. She loudly informed Amalia and Ayleen that she had signed up because it was cheaper than rehab. She snuck out at night for cigarettes, tamed a mouse and kept it in a shoebox under her bed, flouted the basic restrictions on their dietary intake.

"They don't actually give a shit what we do," she told Amalia and Ayleen, her mouth full of Takis. "They just want bodies to pack into the test voyage. So when they send actual rich colonists, they'll know what not to do to them."

Darcy had no family, it appeared, with her or anywhere. What she did have was an uncanny ability to conjure up intimacy with anyone who drifted into her orbit. She charmed the nurse aides and the janitors. The phlebotomist who took their blood once a month. The counselors who gave them cursory psychiatric evaluations. She was unpredictable and loud but always funny, always remembered small facts about people's families, could spin a private joke out of five minutes of acquaintance. Darcy and Ayleen were immediate friends, bonding through the reliable method of shared complaints. The dining hall was too devoid of hot sauce, the phlebotomist pricked them too many times, the occupants of the other cubicles farted in their sleep.

Amalia watched them without joining, impervious to Darcy's attempts to tease her. Until one day Darcy located her outside the shelter, perched on the wall that surrounded the portable showers. This wall was Amalia's favorite place to retreat; it soaked up the sun, and with the mist and faint hiss of the showers it recalled to her the ocean. Darcy held out to Amalia a plate of scavenged dried fruit, apricots and apples and papaya, each precisely diced and assembled in discrete mounds. Then she held out a fork. "Look, we're stuck in this craphole together." Uninvited, she climbed up on the low wall and crossed her legs, mirroring Amalia. "At least have a meal with me." Darcy made no mention of the weirdness of the food. Amalia looked down at the plate for a moment, lips moving soundlessly. Then she looked up, and smiled.

After four months they all advanced from the primary to secondary selection round, and Darcy claimed this confirmed her theory. After eight months, Ayleen and her parents were accepted as part of the mission manifest, while Darcy and Amalia were rejected. Amalia did not know Darcy's reaction to this, because they departed the shelter without seeing each other again. Whether this was by coincidence or mutual resolve, the outcome was the same.

Amalia offers Vine a peach, and has to explain to them about the pit. The expression on their face as they bite down is otherworldly. She sets the child up with World Cup 2039 and takes Darcy on a tour of the house. Leading her old friend down the hallway, Amalia feels like a kid again, a trespasser in someone else's beautiful life. And then every few minutes she comes back into herself, remembers, this is *mine*, and is filled with joy.

In the kitchen Darcy reaches up to touch a copper saucepan hanging from the overhead rack. She pauses like this, arm outstretched, fingers brushing the gleaming metal. Amalia might burst. *Look at me*, she imagines this pot says to Darcy, *I made it. There were no guarantees, but I'm okay.* The whole house, she is aware, has been constructed to bellow out this message, though generally she is unsure whose fears she hopes to allay. She has no watchful family eyes to chart her ascension or decline. She pictures Darcy, surrounded by fellow organizers and a warren of children they have salvaged, all gathered together eating some kind of warm candlelit stew. This gives her a jolt of something vicious: heat lightning at her core muted by dense clouds. Outwardly she widens her smile.

"Those are Erik's grandmother's. Wedding gift. And see, we did the countertops in stained concrete. Erik poured them himself." She slides a hand over the smooth, cool surface of the counter. "I'm so into the rustic these days." She skips over to the ceramic double sink, pulls the faucet on and then off, just to watch a perfect ribbon of water emerge, vanish. She spins to Darcy as though she has just performed a magic trick, holds both palms up and out. The whole house is an offering.

Darcy smiles. "Very impressive."

"Oh, stop. It's just so nice to have a project. Like, I love rural life, but sometimes I'm so bored I could throw myself under a tractor, you know?" She giggles.

"Right." Darcy fingers the lapels of her denim vest.

Amalia is aware of the distance separating them. How far Darcy would have to reach in order to touch her. There was something between them once: a kind of speaking without fear of being misunderstood, a lifting of the veil. They both strain to recall it, but that time is so distant it might as well be in another dimension. Maybe their memories are wrong and it never existed. Or maybe, if they enact the right gestures, recite the right litanies, they can regain it. Like dredging up a language lost in childhood.

These questions swim at great depths, while on the surface they press on through the thicket of pleasantries.

Darcy says, "I'm, uh. I'm so sorry about the farm."

"No, no. You think I hate it? I know, I never pictured me as a farm girl either, back when we wore those paper gowns all the time. But honestly, it's invigorating."

"But the fields?"

"Oh!" Amalia realizes what she means. "Oh, no, those are intentionally fallow." She is struck by a gust of embarrassment. Though she knows little about cultivation herself it becomes important that Darcy not see the farm—no, the business—no, the *family*—as inept. "Of course if they were irrigated we could plant them. But we're selling our claim to the water this year. It's a more solid investment than cultivation. It's not like we're trapped in some dust bowl. I mean, it is a dust bowl. But we're doing great. We're fine." She does not speak about the storms that break over the rock-hard earth, that strip the fields of soil and leave the sides of their house caked in fine gray mud. She does not speak about chiseling the clay from their windows, and watching new seedlings drown in the soup.

Darcy looks as though she's just noticed Amalia. "I should have realized."

"How could you? Water markets are so *dull*. Nothing as exciting as your life, I'm sure. Are you still, uh, volunteering?"

"Organizing."

"Organizing! Of course."

"Well, I have a social work license now, so I guess that's different." Darcy hunches her shoulders and shoves her hands deep in her pockets as she says this. Amalia, scholar of affect, applauds this performance of humility. Darcy continues, "But basically the same. I've been at the Parma settlement since we left the center."

"Ten years! That's incredible."

"It's rare. People burn out. I'm kind of the institutional memory of the place."

"That must be so rewarding."

Darcy uncoils. "I'm not doing it for a reward."

Amalia feels a flash of irritation. She has walked into a setup. "No, I didn't mean—"

"I'm doing it because there are three hundred refugees arriving from the coasts every day. Companies run caravans from Florida, from California, from the Chesapeake. They take people's money and dump them at the Ohio border. No information, no supplies. We don't have sanitation for that many people. We still don't have electricity."

As Darcy talks, Amalia grows impatient. As though she needs a lecture on the world she was a part of only a decade ago. All at once everything about Darcy feels too familiar. Her patched vest and cutoffs, her laser-focused righteousness. Her ability to have thought through everything a little more thoroughly than you, and to have chosen a slightly more selfless response. Amalia feels weary and sorry for her friend, frozen in sanctimonious post-adolescence.

"I'm in youth services," Darcy continues. "We work with children who get to the settlement without families. We're trying to get a school started. Right now we cook meals, take them to doctor's appointments, give them a place to sleep."

"Like a family."

"Well, no, like foster care in a refugee camp. Right now our biggest need is lice combs. People are always donating clothes. Like, thanks, lady, like we need all your old bras."

She paces as she talks, runs her fingers the length of the island countertop. Amalia sinks onto one of the upholstered benches in the breakfast nook. The sun is dropping into afternoon; the light through the window is the faint green of the thunderheads over distant fields. They build and build and never break. Nothing hums or flits through the air. Nothing burrows or churns or decomposes in the soil. Somewhere, distantly, kale grown in hydroponic towers is being priced like gold. Somewhere even more distant, refugee boats linger in the Gulf. Somewhere, else-where, humanity seethes, but not here.

Amalia tries to recover her position. "I should have reached out to you. I'm embarrassed about that."

"I understand why you didn't," Darcy says. "You're trying to make this new life for yourself. It's weird if parts of the old life come drifting in."

"That's not it–" But she breaks off, because that's exactly it, and her denial sounds implausible. "It's more like–"

Darcy brushes this away. "I didn't talk to anyone the first year. I spent so much time thinking about how to survive on another planet, I didn't think about what it would be like to survive on this one."

"Did you really think there was a chance you could leave?"

"No, I thought it was a scam. A warm bed for nine months while they ran tests." Darcy pauses. "I guess part of me really thought maybe I'd get to leave."

Darcy scrutinizes Amalia with an expression that Amalia cannot parse. She stands too quickly, bruises her thigh on the table edge. "Do you want tea?"

Darcy says, "Do you blame yourself?

"What?"

Darcy inhales, chews her lip for a moment, considering. "When they rejected me from the trial, I didn't think I would feel anything. I thought I knew it was coming, but I also really thought they were just searching for bodies. So when I got kicked off it was like, wow, you're not even qualified to be human trash."

Amalia barely shakes her head, as though she is afraid of big motions. "That's not what it meant."

"Yeah, I know." Darcy shrugs. "I got over it. I had plenty of reasons to hate myself, couldn't take on another one." She watches Amalia sideways.

Looking into the sink, Amalia says, "You always seemed so confident."

Darcy makes a dismissive noise in her throat. "I was a fucking eighteen-year-old punk. I had no idea what I wanted."

Amalia seeks a diplomatic phrasing for her question. "Do you know what you want now?"

Darcy fixes Amalia with a bulldog stare. Later, Amalia will think back to this look and realize she was steeling herself to do what she had come here to do. But she doesn't know that now.

"I want to do the work. I want to build with the people left here. I want people to have more than a tarp over their heads. I want to figure out how to feed everyone."

Amalia snorts. "You could work on that until you're dead."

"I'm not looking for an end. I'm just looking to do the work." She repeats this phrase like a devotion. Amalia watches her friend in profile. Darcy is still curled into the elastic body of a punk, but edging toward age. The brief shock of hair at the top of her head: is it held by product or its own grime? Darcy belongs to an aesthetic that hovers just outside the threshold of fashion. Fashion changes with the season, but Darcy's studied, performative counterculture has held constant for the past seventy years. Amalia, who has spent the past decade hauling herself up the ladder, swapping out her vocabulary, her clothing, her likes and dislikes, finds herself subtly repelled by Darcy. *You want to give your life for something that will never be achieved; where is the strength in that?* As soon as this thought enters her mind it is replaced by remorse. Darcy's presence is an unexpected opportunity, she tells herself. She thought she had closed off her past so thoroughly that no one would slip through. But here is a chance to have her new self measured against the old. To have someone see how far she has come.

She clears her throat. "I know what you mean. Erik and I put together a benefit every year. I'm on the board of his family's foundation. I think, if I weren't here, I wouldn't get to do any of these things."

"You're so generous," Darcy murmurs with scant inflection.

The shelter contracted with a genome company to calculate the risk of the remaining six hundred candidates. Amalia, Darcy, and four hundred eighteen others were disqualified as holding too many potential inherited disorders. They were not told what these were. They received a stipend for their time and were asked to vacate the facility in forty-eight hours.

Ayleen, Amalia, and their parents sat in the cubicle, and their father explained what would happen. "We would not do this if it were not best for all of us, do you understand?" He spoke too quickly, as though he were reciting a memorized speech at double speed. "There's nothing we could do for either of you if we stayed."

That evening, the sisters stood side by side and looked at themselves in the bathroom mirror. Their nearly identical bodies. Ayleen a year older, Amalia an inch taller, or she would be if she didn't hunch, but they had never had a reason to think of themselves as separate before. Now, though, someone had peered inside them and revealed, twined into the cores of their cells, the thing that would split them from each other. Sunder them by thirty-four million miles.

Amalia asked, "Are you scared?"

Ayleen answered, "No. I'm worried about you."

"Don't be. I'm going to start a new life. It's you I'm scared for."

"I'm adaptable. I'll be fine."

They each pressed their fingers to their faces, stretched the skin around their eyes, tried to imagine themselves growing old, and failed.

She did not go to watch the shuttle depart. On the day of the launch, she left the mission complex for a diner on the outskirts of town. She glanced at her phone and noted the launch time, just as her tofu scramble and iced tea were set down. She marked the moment with a single inhalation. And then felt nothing except hunger.

In that moment the substance of her beliefs, once molten and fluid, hardened into glass. Your future was the product of the choices you made, and nothing else. No matter how much it might feel possible, there was no such thing as escape. Everything was so clear. You made your life exactly where you were. You had no one but yourself.

She took the divestment payout and enrolled in a two-year business management program. In school she found there were people for whom the world was not changing, for whom the landscape and weather were interesting phenomena to observe, rather than vengeful forces. She was fascinated by these people. Her desire to understand them amounted to a physical hunger, a throbbing in her gut. They looked like her, in thrifted sweaters and ripped jeans, but inside they held an alien stillness, while her body held only threat and abandon. She saw that it was not this constancy that made them so assured, but their assurance that created constancy. She would make herself like them. She watched them from a distance at first, then gradually began speaking to them, after class, in bars, in line for the watery powdered drink the school tried to pass off as coffee. She practiced their cadences and their slang. She mastered the art of never revealing more than necessary. That people might see through her charade, might view her displaced status as an attractively exotic quality, did not occur to her. That people might genuinely care for her, and wish to relate to her regardless of her background, was irrelevant.

Eventually she met Erik, the final test in her journey toward self-transformation. She passed. He wanted to bring her home. His family squinted, but abided. When she married him, she married into an agricultural dynasty, people who had thrown their lot into evading the shifts of the world rather than adapting.

The refugee resettlement companies acquired more and more land, grew into massive, unincorporated shantytowns, and Amalia learned how to order in restaurants, how to show a bartender she knew what she was talking about. Chocolate and citrus and almonds grew endangered, then extinct in grocery stores, and Amalia learned which cafés were best for a weekday lunch. The requirements to travel into cities became more and more stringent, checkpoints were erected, ID surveillance implemented, and Amalia learned how to manage a savings account, how to negotiate with real estate agents. The media coverage drifted away from the suburbs, the riots, the fires, the floods, zoomed in on elegant, exclusive city centers, and Amalia learned how to relax, ease in, sink down into the growing buffer of security and comfort around her.

She did not search for Darcy. With each step forward in her life she felt that she was evading something, staying just out of reach of the floodwaters roaring down a dry riverbed. Finding Darcy, she felt, though she never articulated this to herself, might cause her to stumble, to be caught in the oncoming torrent and dragged under.

*   *   *

The sun is sinking lower. Power lines and dead tree snags cast long shadows over the empty fields. They check on Vine in the game room, immersed in holographic fútbol. Amalia watches the child, diving to block a goal, tumbling onto the soft foam floor.

"They seem to be feeling better," Amalia says.

Darcy nods cautiously. "It comes and goes."

"What's wrong with them?" Amalia asks, then grimaces; the words come out more harshly than she intended. Darcy shakes her head, pointing her chin at Vine as though the child might hear. Amalia thinks this is unlikely; inside Vine's helmet they are center forward in a packed, cheering stadium. But she acquiesces.

"Do you want to see the garden?" Amalia bites her lip as she asks. She loves her garden. If Darcy shows no interest she's not sure how she will bear it. But Darcy is pliant, follows Amalia behind the house to the curving permaculture beds she has painstakingly raised, sage and mugwort, monarda and thyme. The silvery greens and purples stand out, soft and lush, in stark contrast to the harsh and empty fields.

She flicks the pollinator switch so that minuscule drones buzz from plant to plant, weighing down the bee balm flowerheads. This makes the scene feel complete to her. Erik was reluctant to install the garden until she demonstrated to him that it could be irrigated entirely from dew catchers, diverting nothing from their water allotment.

Amalia pinches a fuzzy leaf and crushes it. "Scented geranium, smell!" She holds it toward Darcy. "Real lemon, right?"

Darcy takes the leaf and crushes it more thoroughly so her finger pads are stained green. "That's nice." Then folds and tears and crushes again.

Amalia lets the silence stretch before asking, "Why are you watching Vine?"

"They just got here a week ago. From Norfolk. Came in on a boat that was picking people out of the sea off the coast of the Carolinas. No family. Somewhere in there, they got caught in a boat propeller. Tore up their back."

"Oh god. Poor thing."

"There's MRSA in the camp. The cuts got infected."

"So glad the game room is padded!"

Darcy works the leaf to a pulp. "They're tough. We have herbs, we pack the wound with silver. We can control the infection, but it doesn't go away."

Amalia shudders. Occasionally some information drifts in to remind her that the world is a churning soup of disease and misery. The forty thousand acres of dead earth form a moat that keeps her oasis safe. A single different choice could have left her like Vine, adrift, her body undefended.

Darcy is licking the pulped leaf from her fingers. "They need phage therapy, but we don't have access to that."

Amalia kneels to check the irrigation hose that winds through the garden bed. A porous black tube, half buried, steadily leaches water, keeping the soil damp and dark and fragrant. Amalia buries her hand in the moist earth for just a moment, lets herself sigh. Darcy watches her, inhaling deeply, and Amalia imagines she is finding some peace from the square of fertile earth. She is gratified when Darcy says, "This really is beautiful."

"Isn't it? Whenever people say we should move to the city, I tell them about this. No space for this inside the limit."

"You could move, though?"

"Oh, definitely. We have access visas. We could probably jump the housing line if we wanted. Erik knows people. But he says this is what he grew up with. It's so peaceful out here. And I agree, of course."

"What does an access visa get you?"

"Better shopping! And, hmm, health centers. Grocery stores, ironically. I used to be able to order everything, but now deliveries take so long! Like we don't matter if we don't live in the city limits."

"You're not the only ones." Darcy plucks another geranium leaf. Held up to the sun, it glows a translucent yellow. "Who do you sell water rights to?"

Amalia thinks. "Oh, resettlement companies, mostly. Sometimes the city. There's so much demand for water! It's really wonderful to feel like we're helping. It is."

"Doesn't it put you at a disadvantage? If other farms grow things and you don't?"

"We all do it. Anyone who's a significant landholder. We have a cost-share agreement, so everyone reduces yield by the same percentage." She laughs. "It's ridiculously complex, but so beautifully designed. Erik's dad is on the oversight committee; he does such a good job."

"What percentage, this year?"

Amalia feels a tug of reluctance before she speaks. "One–one hundred."

"You didn't grow anything?"

"Of course we couldn't say no when the need for water is so great. Those poor people. Well, of course you know."

"You made all your money selling water to the migrant settlements?"

She sees Darcy's eyes flick around the lush, lively garden bed. She thinks of Darcy taking in the gleaming new kitchen, the bookshelves, the game room. She has been letting her guard down, feeling proud of herself, of the family, their generosity. But she has a sudden flash of what is happening in Darcy's mind, different from what she envisioned, and she is unmoored by the disparity.

"Look, I–I know everything seems great here, but it hasn't been easy. The shift from cultivation is so strange. You lose your identity."

Darcy looks up sharply at her, as though slapped back from a trance. "Identity. Yes."

"Erik's family still doesn't accept me. It doesn't matter how much I do, I'll always be a fugee to them."

"I'm sure they love you. They get to congratulate themselves on how diverse their family is."

Amalia feels a sting behind her eyes. She waits until it passes. She holds all the muscles of her face very still so she can say evenly, "Why did you come find me?"

Darcy continues to stare at Amalia, a fine haze of dust glittering on the bridge of her nose. "Do you wish you could do something really meaningful?"

There is the whisper again, hissing: *Say no*. But maybe this is the gap, the glimmer she has waited for. What will she do with it? "Honestly. I was so glad you called. Maybe I'm losing my mind? You think it's ridiculous, I can tell. It's not noble and action-packed like your life." She's starting to wander, she's losing sight of what she's talking about. She senses that her chance to confess something of consequence, to reveal her own crystalline heart, is slipping away.

They both transfer their gazes to the geranium plant, so Amalia misses the expression on Darcy's face before she speaks, the cast of dread replaced by grim resolve. "I need to ask you something."

The sun is at her back now, and Amalia imagines herself illuminated like the leaf. "Anything!"

"I need you to get Vine into the city on your visa. And we need money, to start them on treatment for the infection."

A cloud blots out the light. Amalia laughs, "What?"

Darcy blinks repeatedly. "I don't know anyone else to ask."

"That's ridiculous. I'm sure you have lots of people."

"We don't."

All around Amalia the world is resizing itself. Things once very distant grow rapidly near. "I haven't seen you in ten years."

"I know. I'm asking because you know how it was. You still know."

"How much?"

"Ten thousand dollars. To start."

"My god. Look, I don't know what impression you get from all this, but we actually aren't so well-off. I haven't told you half of what's going on with the land—"

Darcy murmurs, dully, "We'd pay it back."

This makes Amalia laugh. "Don't be ridiculous. I know what it's like—"

Darcy pounces, "And that's why I'm asking you."

"But—Vine's not registered. It's against the law." Amalia feels stupid as she says this, a child threatening to tell the teacher.

"The law!" Darcy says it with such disdain that Amalia believes she has sworn.

"No. No, don't 'fuck the law' me. I'm not some teenager looking to rebel. I have a life. I have a house."

"It's not a crime spree."

"It might as well be. To the people I'm around. You think they don't know how many people are trying to get in? You think they don't get asked things like this all the time?"

"Well then, that's the fucking crime spree."

"Stop swearing."

"No." Darcy is ignited. "They fucking put all the resources in cities and wall them off with checkpoints and visa cams. It's fucking medieval."

"I'm not Robin Hood! Darcy. God. You came here to argue idealism? We're adults now."

"So we can do something about it."

"You're asking me to do something that could end me. What about all the good I do from a place like this? You don't know everything Erik's family does."

"Oh, do they have a grant program? Do they do *dinners?*" With her pretensions to civility cast off, Darcy looks smaller and darker than before, like a bullet. The dirt on her vest collar is visible. The rashes down the sides of her neck. The lead in her eyes. She says, "You haven't changed. I think this was always exactly who you wanted to be."

Amalia is activated by this outrage, by the clear afternoon light. The sap surges in her, stretches her toward the sun. "You think I'm not trapped, too? We're all trapped. Maybe, when things get really bad–"

"Things are bad *now*. Things are really fucking *awful*."

A soft clack. Vine has come out into the garden. Amalia sees how small they are in their oversized T-shirt. Their knobbly joints and sticklike limbs. They set the VR headset down on the patio table. "I won." Their eyes bounce between the two adults and then they go and curl their body against Darcy. "Are you okay?"

"Yeah, sweetie, I'm fine." Darcy hugs with warmth but restraint.

Amalia has an image of the state-of-the-art padding in her game room covered in pus, pulsing with unconquerable infection.

Vine mouths, "I want another peach."

Darcy is about to say no, but Amalia swoops in, herds the child back to the kitchen. "Have two peaches, sweetie. Have as many as you want."

Vine holds a fruit in each hand, looking bewildered.

Darcy comes to the kitchen doorway, emotions fighting in her face. "We're going to leave soon, Vine. Get ready."

With peach juice dripping down their chin, Vine whines in protest.

Amalia hands them a cloth and a container. "Don't worry. You have time for one more match. Wipe your hands first."

Vine skips back to the game room, shaking their hands dry.

Darcy watches them don the helmet, says, "You're really generous, when it costs you nothing."

"No, I'm generous when I can afford it. There's a difference. You were always trying to give everything of yourself away, even back then. You end up with nothing."

Darcy is out of the doorway, across the kitchen, closer to Amalia than she has been. "You're going to talk about how we were back then?"

Amalia's mouth is dry. "We were both naive."

"I was naive. You were–ruthless. I had no idea. So maybe you're right, maybe I'm still stupid."

Amalia is backed up against the sink. She can feel the counter jutting into the small of her back. There is something like fear in her, though she barely remembers what that feels like.

Darcy has been looking somewhere in the middle distance, and now her eyes refocus on Amalia. "You know, I still think about how we were, sometimes."

"Oh, stop." Amalia laughs. "Don't be desperate. Are you trying to flirt with me? When we both know–" She has nothing to finish this sentence with, so she stops.

"What?" Darcy asks, and the silence stretches. Finally Amalia pushes away from the counter. As she expected, Darcy falls back and lets her pass.

Amalia pretends to watch Vine score a goal. "Why this kid? You must work with hundreds of kids."

Darcy rakes her hair, looking vaguely revolted with herself. She looks helplessly into the game room. "They don't have anyone."

"That's true of all of them, though. Why–"

"Why not?" The blade of Darcy's tone belies the breezy words.

"You're asking me to risk my livelihood for *why not?*"

"As if it really matters. 'Why this kid?' As if that would change your answer." Darcy settles awkwardly onto a bench seat, making no more effort to look comfortable.

Amalia watches the tense, clouded clot of a person who has manifested in her kitchen. "You see yourself in them." She intends for this to sound perceptive, but it comes out mocking.

Darcy looks desolate. She says, "I'm sorry."

Amalia identifies the sourness in her gut. She is appalled, she realizes. She is most appalled by Darcy's approach, the blunt unadorned demand. If only Darcy had asked a different way, then maybe she could have been more receptive. She sees herself as an intricate and delicate puzzle box, undone only through the perfect alignment of elements. A rivulet of sadness enters her heart, composed of this regret. There must have been a way of asking that would have made it easy for her to say yes. She loves to be generous. But this demand—as abrupt as getting mugged—to this, unfortunately, absolutely, she has to say no.

"I'm not brave like you, Darcy." She intends this to be kind, and to be the end. Briskly, she walks to the entrance, out to the front patio. She knows Darcy will follow her. People follow when you lead. Darcy's footsteps come behind her, soft on the flagstone. Amalia folds her arms tightly across her stomach and looks across the fields. Dirt queen. "I'll call you a car."

There is a silence while Amalia swipes the phone. There used to be swallows that dipped and tittered over these fields, but in their absence Amalia has grown used to the rushing of the air and nothing else. Darcy scratches her neck, twists her fingers, seems to be at the edge of another decision.

"I only asked because I thought you might—"

"Well, you thought incorrectly. But it's fine. My signal isn't working, hold on."

"—I thought you might say yes, because of what you did for Amalia."

The sound of her own name freezes the whole scene. Stems bowed by the breeze do not straighten. Pollinator drones hang in the air.

"What?"

"I know your little sister is the one who got disqualified. I know you let her take your place on the ship. And you took her name."

"What—"

"I know that was brave. *That's* why I'm asking you."

"What are you talking about?"

"Ayleen—"

"You are insane. I need you to leave."

"Amalia was the first person I was in love with. It's insane to think I wouldn't notice."

"They left me!" The words burst out with less control than she intends. The foundation of her identity is liquefying beneath her. "There's nothing else to know. They left. That's it."

"I'm sorry, Ayleen."

"Why are you calling me that?"

"I never told anybody."

"You need to get out." Resolutely, she–*Amalia*–reaches out with both hands to tug back the limits of herself. "Now."

Darcy stands at the edge of the porch, as though she is about to depart. "But what would happen, if someone found out?"

There is not much, hardly any, but just enough of an edge in Darcy's voice that Amalia regains herself at once. The blinding cloud of panic that has engulfed her gives way to calm and clarity.

"Oh. You're blackmailing me."

Darcy shakes her head vigorously. "No."

"With an insane, unfounded lie. You're trying to blackmail me into helping you with your sad welfare case."

"I just asked you a question, Ayleen."

"Stop calling me that."

"I should leave." Darcy puts one foot down on the step but still watches Amalia.

Amalia's phone buzzes to inform them that a car is on its way. Amalia pockets the phone with shaking hands. She feels all the metal hatches of her body slamming shut. She knows how to make herself impenetrable to danger. She plays along. "I have no idea what would happen. Nothing. It's fraud."

"If someone reported that they knew of a family who defrauded the company. A passenger on the ship with unverified credentials. It could invalidate the whole experiment."

"They wouldn't invalidate it. Too many funds sunk into one project."

"They'd have to recover those funds somehow. They'd go after participants."

This is funny, actually. Amalia sees the humor. "You're trying to scare me by threatening my family. But it's a family I haven't spoken to in ten years. They left. They don't affect me anymore."

"Did you ever try to get in touch?"

"No."

"Bullshit. I did. I wrote her down here, when I thought you were her. Then I wrote her up there, when I realized she was you."

"That doesn't make any sense."

Something in Darcy comes loose. "God, don't insult me. I found her things to eat. I talked her through panic attacks. I gave her a place to sleep when you and your parents were screaming at each other." She clutches her hair with both hands. "Don't tell me I don't remember."

"There's lots of things you don't remember."

"How did you do it? How did you pull it off?"

"We didn't pull anything off."

"But how did you keep anyone from noticing that Amalia was—"

"Amalia is here. *Me*."

Darcy takes a deep breath, turns to face Amalia fully. "You can say whatever you want. I know you gave her your chance to go. And then you made a life out of nothing. Like we all do. That's how I know you're brave. That's why I'm asking. But if that doesn't work, then yes, I'm blackmailing you."

Amalia watches her coldly, and realizes with perfect clarity that no matter what Darcy threatens, she can say no. There is not actually anything that can touch her. She holds her life together with the fury of her desire. The house, with its gracious fixtures and sun-filled rooms. The husband and the evenings in the city and the refuge from floods and fires and blackouts. Darcy will never have this, because Darcy spills her desire carelessly on others who wander across her path. Darcy's methods of desiring are incomprehensible to her, and thus do not exist, are no threat.

She says, "It wasn't brave. It was obvious. It was safer for her to go live in a pod on another planet than to stay here. What does that say?"

Darcy smiles a little sadly. "I would have given her my spot, too, if I had one. I would have done anything."

Amalia almost laughs. "In the end she just walked on, with my ID. They didn't check. You were right. They didn't care who we were."

Vine cracks open the front door, joins them on the porch. They writhe inside their shirt. "I'm *itchy*."

Darcy starts. "We need to change their bandages. Repack the wounds."

The car is still ten minutes away. Amalia retrieves the first aid kit, shows the two of them to the bathroom.

There is no voice in her head anymore. No whispers guide her. She imagines herself as her family would see her. Dirt queen. Twenty-eight years running from floods. She rules the waters now. They flow where she points. The money runs to her and pools around her ankles. Her family chose her to leave behind, and they were right. She is safest when alone. Erik loves her, of course, but it's a partnership. She completes his vision of himself. No one has ever reached out to care for her with no thought for anything in return.

She looks at Darcy down the hallway, leaning over Vine, whispering something so that Vine giggles. She feels a glimmer of something bright in the distance. A door cracking open at the far end of a vast dark room. The light that might stream in will not illuminate, it will incinerate her. She doesn't know what of herself will remain.

There is no precise moment when she makes a decision. No leap off a precipice. Looking back she will swear she is the same person in the moment before and the moment after. Her beliefs do not change. You make your life with what you have. You have nothing but yourself. Again and again, impossible things become quotidian without a sound or a tremor.

She takes a breath and tears her eyes from them. She runs to the master bedroom, rummages through Erik's dresser. She returns to the bathroom threshold with her arms full. Alone, on an inhospitable planet, with strangers in her harbor, she speaks. "The clinic opens at eight. We can go first thing in the morning. We should expect at least two hours to get through the checkpoint. So you should sleep here. I don't know if you brought pajamas but I can lend you some of Erik's shirts, would that be alright?"

She holds up a stretched-out Cleveland Browns jersey, and a threadbare TRANS IS BEAUTIFUL T-shirt.

Darcy does not look surprised or grateful. She nods curtly, and snaps on nitrile gloves. Vine points to the T-shirt. "I want that one."

* * *

When the car arrives, they send it away back down the dusty road. Outside the sun is setting, and the fields glow so golden they almost appear to contain life. Distantly, Amalia hears the garage door open, and Erik's car slides inside. She plans what she will say to him. In the bathroom Vine sits on the toilet lid, knees against their chest. Darcy says, "I need to check the bandages," and Vine obediently lifts their shirt.

Peel away the tape, the white gauze, the sheets of silver foil. The wounds beneath are raw red, edged in yellow pus, creeping all across Vine's back. An archipelago of wounds. The map of a drowned world.

Here and now, they tend that world with the gentleness of their hands. The hushed tones of their voices. They make a shelter of words and small gestures. Of course it is not enough, the waters are rising to wash it away like twigs, and yet they make it again and again. For a long moment Amalia's eyes drift closed and she sees, against the black of her eyelids, bright threads coursing with silver light. The threads run between the three of them and within them and around them and into the walls of the house and out the windows into the earth. Amalia inhales at the sight and opens her eyes, and finds the world illuminated by only the fluorescent bulb of her bathroom. She closes her eyes again, but nothing is there.

You can do it, you know. There is nothing here that needs doing that cannot be done. It is easier than you think. It is possible to resurrect the words that have been forgotten. It is possible to live without shame.

Amalia fills the sink with warm water. She passes Darcy a knitted washcloth lathered with goat's-milk soap. Together they wash the child's back. Darcy dabs around the edge of each wound. The cloth eases away the yellow crust and rusty scabs, blots up fresh blood as it begins to flow. Vine grits their teeth and twists their fingers in their shirt hem, but doesn't even whimper as the soap touches raw flesh. Amalia takes the cloth from Darcy when it is saturated and rinses it in the sink. She wrings it out, returns it, rinses it again and again, until the clear water in the basin is suffused with red.

Mikael Awake is a writer based in Brooklyn, NY, and the child of formerly undocumented immigrants from Ethiopia. His essays have appeared in *GQ*, the *Common*, *Bookforum*, the *Awl*, and elsewhere.

Asja Bakić is a Bosnian/Croatian author. Her debut short story collection, *Mars*, was published by Feminist Press earlier this year. She's currently finishing her next book of short stories, *Sladostrašće*.

Birna Anna Björnsdóttir is an Icelandic writer who lives in New York City and Reykjavík. She is the author of three novels. Her most recent one is *Perlan*, published in Iceland in 2017.

Claire G. Coleman is a Wirlomin Noongar poet, essayist, novelist, and speaker, whose ancestral country is in the south coast of Western Australia. Her debut novel, *Terra Nullius*, won a black&write! Writing Fellowship and a Norma K Hemming award and was shortlisted for the Stella Prize and Aurealis Awards, among many others. *The Old Lie* (September 2019) is her second novel.

Rachel Heng is the author of the novel *Suicide Club* (Henry Holt, 2018), which was featured as a best summer read by outlets such as the *Irish Times*, *ELLE*, *Gizmodo*, *NYLON*, the *Rumpus*, and *Bustle*. *Suicide Club* will be translated into ten languages worldwide and was shortlisted for the Gladstone's Library Writer in Residence award in 2019. Rachel's short fiction has received a Pushcart Prize Special Mention and Prairie Schooner's Jane Geske Award, and has appeared or is forthcoming in *Glimmer Train*, *Guernica*, *Kenyon Review*, *Best Singaporean Short Stories Volume Four*, and elsewhere. She has received grants and fellowships from the Vermont Studio Center, Sewanee Writers' Conference, Fine Arts Work Center, and the National Arts Council of Singapore. Rachel is currently a fellow at the Michener Center for Writers.

Tommy Orange's debut novel, *There There*, won the 2018 PEN/America Hemingway Award and was a finalist for the Pulitzer Prize in fiction. Orange is an enrolled member of the Cheyenne and Arapaho Tribes of Oklahoma. He was born and raised in Oakland, California.

Abbey Mei Otis is a writer, a teaching artist, a storyteller, and a firestarter, raised in the woods of North Carolina. She loves people and art forms on the margins. Her debut story collection, *Alien Virus Love Disaster* (Small Beer Press), was a finalist for the 2019 Philip K. Dick Award and the Neukom Institute Literary Arts Award For Speculative Fiction.

Elif Shafak is an award-winning novelist and the most widely read female author in Turkey. She has written seventeen books, eleven of which are novels, including the Booker Prize-nominated *10 Minutes 38 Seconds in this Strange World*. Translated into fifty languages, Shafak is a political scientist, a women's rights and LGBT rights activist, and a two-time TED Global speaker. An honorary fellow at St Anne's College, Oxford, she has been awarded the title of Chevalier des Arts et des Lettres, and she is a member of the Royal Society of Literature.

Kanishk Tharoor is the author of *Swimmer Among the Stars* (FSG, 2017), a collection of short stories that was a *Guardian* Book of the Year and an *NPR* Book of the Year, and which won the Tata Lit Live! First Book Award for fiction in India. His writing has appeared in the *New York Times*, the *Atlantic*, the *Guardian*, the *Paris Review*, the *New Yorker*, *Virginia Quarterly Review*, and elsewhere, and has been nominated for a National Magazine Award. He is the presenter of the BBC radio series *Museum of Lost Objects* and a senior editor at *Foreign Affairs*.

Luis Alberto Urrea is the author of eighteen books, including *The House of Broken Angels*, a 2018 finalist for the NBCC Award in fiction. A Guggenheim Fellow and Pulitzer Prize finalist, he has also won an Edgar Award, an American Academy of Arts and Letters Award, a Lannan Literary Award, and an American Book Award, among others. Born in Tijuana to an American mother and Mexican father, Urrea is most known as a border writer, though he is much more interested in bridges. He is a distinguished professor of creative writing at the University of Illinois at Chicago.

Jennifer Zoble teaches writing and translation in the Liberal Studies program at NYU, co-edits InTranslation at the *Brooklyn Rail*, co-produces the international audio drama podcast *Play for Voices*, and translates Bosnian/Croatian/Serbian- and Spanish-language literature. Her translation of *Mars* by Asja Bakić was published by Feminist Press in 2019.

The Natural Resources Defense Council (NRDC)
works to safeguard the Earth—its people, its
plants and animals, and the natural systems on
which all life depends. At the core of its mission
is a simple idea: a healthy environment should
be a basic right for all of us—regardless of where
we live, how we vote, or what we look like.
NRDC creates solutions for lasting environmental
change by combining the power of more than 3
million members and online activists with the
expertise of over 600 scientists, lawyers, and
policy advocates. The organization engages in
a variety of arts and cultural partnerships to
engage the public on critical environmental
issues. To learn more about how NRDC is tack-
ling the climate crisis, visit *nrdc.org/climate* or
contact NRDC at *nrdcinfo@nrdc.org*.

TAKE ACTION

NRDC has offices in New York City; Washington, D.C.; Los Angeles; San Francisco; Chicago; Bozeman, MT; and Beijing. Learn more at *nrdc.org/get-involved* and follow us on social media.

WAYS TO SUPPORT THE NRDC

All donations to NRDC are tax-deductible and your gift will help defend our environment on all fronts, combat climate change, and fight to restore the natural ecosystems such as our forests, that we all so desperately depend on. You can make a donation at *nrdc.org/donate*.

An investigation of surveillance in the digital age, with
special advisor the Electronic Frontier Foundation

In our first-ever entirely nonfiction issue of McSweeney's, *The End of Trust* (McSweeney's 54) features more than thirty writers and artists investigating surveillance in the digital age. Across more than 350 pages of essays, debates, interviews, graphs, and manifestos from over thirty contributors–including Edward Snowden, Julia Angwin, Malkia Cyril, Gabriella Coleman, Jenna Wortham, and dozens more, and with special advisor Electronic Frontier Foundation–this monumental collection asks whether we've reached the end of trust, and whether we even care.

> **"I couldn't put down Keep Scrolling Till You Feel Something
> but then the sheer weight of this massive book ripped off both of my arms."**
> —Chad Nackers, Editor-in-Chief of *The Onion*

Join us as we revisit the first twenty-one years of McSweeney's Internet Tendency, from our bright-eyed and bewildered early stages to our world-weary and bewildered recent days. *Keep Scrolling Till You Feel Something* is a coming-of-age celebration of the pioneering website, featuring brand-new pieces and hundreds of classics by some of today's best humor writers, like Ellie Kemper, Wendy Molyneux, Jesse Eisenberg, Tim Carvell, Karen Chee, Colin Nissan, and many more.

Available now from McSweeney's

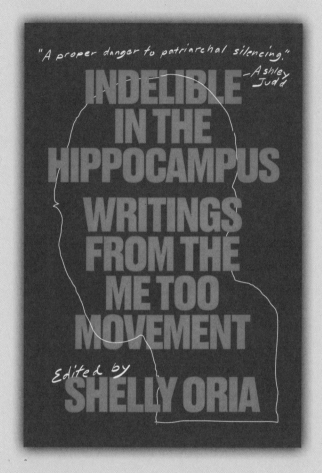

"This book is a proper danger to patriarchal silencing."
–Ashley Judd

Among the first books to emerge from the #MeToo movement, *Indelible in the Hippocampus* is a truly intersectional collection of essays, fiction, and poetry. These original texts sound the voices of black, Latinx, Asian, queer, and trans writers, and say "me too" twenty-three times. Together, these pieces create a portrait of cultural sea-change, offering the reader a deeper understanding of this complex, galvanizing pivot in contemporary consciousness.

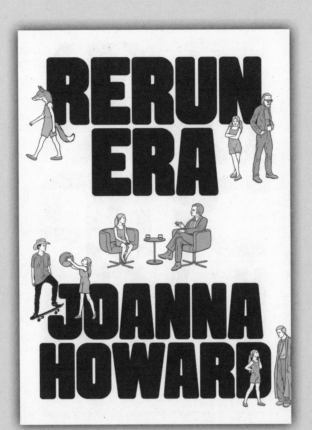

"*A story of time, family, culture, and subjectivity we all need to read, written with a wild, quiet, and wide intelligence.*" –Renee Gladman

Rerun Era is a captivating, propulsive memoir about growing up in the environmentally and economically devastated rural flatlands of Oklahoma, the entwinement of personal memory and the memory of popular culture, and a family thrown into trial by lost love and illness that found common ground in the television. Written in stunning lyric prose, *Rerun Era* firmly establishes Howard as an urgent and necessary voice in American letters.

■ *All That is Evident is Suspect: Readings from the Oulipo* edited by Ian Monk and Daniel Levin Becker

Available now from McSweeney's

All That is Evident is Suspect is the first collection in English to offer a life-size picture of the Oulipo in its historical and contemporary incarnations, and the first in any language to represent all of its members (numbering 41 as of April 2018). Combining fiction, poetry, essays and lectures, and never-published internal correspondence– along with the acrobatically constrained writing and complexly structured narratives that have become synonymous with oulipian practice–this volume shows a unique group of thinkers and artists at work and at play, meditating on and subverting the facts of life, love, and the group itself. It's an unprecedentedly intimate and comprehensive glimpse at the breadth and diversity of one of world literature's most vital, adventurous presences.

STORE.MCSWEENEYS.NET

Also available from McSweeney's

FICTION

The Domestic Crusaders .... Wajahat Ali

The Convalescent .... Jessica Anthony

Emmaus .... Alessandro Baricco

Mr. Gwyn .... Alessandro Baricco

Arkansas .... John Brandon

Citrus County .... John Brandon

A Million Heavens .... John Brandon

A Child Again .... Robert Coover

Stepmother .... Robert Coover

One Hundred Apocalypses and Other Apocalypses .... Lucy Corin

Fever Chart .... Bill Cotter

The Parallel Apartments .... Bill Cotter

Sorry to Disrupt the Peace .... Patty Yumi Cottrell

End of I. .... Stephen Dixon

I. .... Stephen Dixon

A Hologram for the King .... Dave Eggers

Understanding the Sky .... Dave Eggers

The Wild Things .... Dave Eggers

You Shall Know Our Velocity .... Dave Eggers

Donald .... Stephen Elliott, Eric Martin

The Boatbuilder .... Daniel Gumbiner

God Says No .... James Hannaham

The Middle Stories .... Sheila Heti

Songbook .... Nick Hornby

Bowl of Cherries .... Millard Kaufman

Misadventure .... Millard Kaufman

Lemon .... Lawrence Krauser

Search Sweet Country .... Kojo Laing

Hot Pink .... Adam Levin
The Instructions .... Adam Levin
The Facts of Winter .... Paul Poissel
Adios, Cowboy .... Olja Savičević
A Moment in the Sun .... John Sayles
Between Heaven and Here .... Susan Straight
All My Puny Sorrows .... Miriam Toews
The End of Love .... Marcos Giralt Torrente
Vacation .... Deb Olin Unferth
The Best of McSweeney's .... Various
Noisy Outlaws, Unfriendly Blobs... .... Various
Fine, Fine, Fine, Fine, Fine .... Diane Williams
Vicky Swanky Is a Beauty .... Diane Williams
My Documents .... Alejandro Zambra

ART AND COMICS

Song Reader .... Beck
The Berliner Ensemble Thanks You All .... Marcel Dzama
It Is Right to Draw Their Fur .... Dave Eggers
Binky Brown Meets the Holy Virgin Mary .... Justin Green
Animals of the Ocean: .... Dr. and Mr. Doris Haggis-on-Whey
In Particular the Giant Squid
Children and the Tundra .... Dr. and Mr. Doris Haggis-on-Whey
Cold Fusion .... Dr. and Mr. Doris Haggis-on-Whey
Giraffes? Giraffes! .... Dr. and Mr. Doris Haggis-on-Whey
Celebrations of Curious Characters .... Ricky Jay
There Are Many of Us .... Spike Jonze
Be a Nose! .... Art Spiegelman
The Clock without a Face .... Gus Twintig
Everything That Rises: A Book of Convergences .... Lawrence Weschler

BOOKS FOR CHILDREN

Here Comes the Cat! .... Frank Asch; Ill. Vladimir Vagin
Benny's Brigade .... Arthur Bradford; Ill. Lisa Hanawalt
Keep Our Secrets .... Jordan Crane
This Bridge Will Not Be Gray .... Dave Eggers; Ill. Tucker Nichols
The Night Riders .... Matt Furie
We Need a Horse .... Sheila Heti; Ill. Clare Rojas
Stories 1, 2, 3, 4 .... Eugène Ionesco
Hang Glider & Mud Mask .... Jason Jägel, Brian McMullen
Symphony City .... Amy Martin

Crabtree .... Jon and Tucker Nichols
Recipe .... Angela and Michaelanne Petrella; Ill. Mike Bertino, Erin Althea
Awake Beautiful Child .... Amy Krouse Rosenthal; Ill. Gracia Lam
Lost Sloth .... J. Otto Seibold
The Expeditioners I .... S.S. Taylor; Ill. Katherine Roy
The Expeditioners II .... S.S. Taylor; Ill. Katherine Roy
Girl at the Bottom of the Sea .... Michelle Tea; Ill. Amanda Verwey
Mermaid in Chelsea Creek .... Michelle Tea; Ill. Jason Polan

NONFICTION

White Girls .... Hilton Als
In My Home There Is No More Sorrow .... Rick Bass
Maps and Legends .... Michael Chabon
Real Man Adventures .... T Cooper
The Pharmacist's Mate and 8 .... Amy Fusselman
Toro Bravo: Stories. Recipes. No Bull. .... John Gorham, Liz Crain
The End of War .... John Horgan
It Chooses You .... Miranda July
The End of Major Combat Operations .... Nick McDonell
Mission Street Food .... Anthony Myint, Karen Leibowitz
At Home on the Range .... Margaret Yardley Potter, Elizabeth Gilbert
Half a Life .... Darin Strauss

VOICE OF WITNESS

Throwing Stones at the Moon: Narratives .... Eds. Sibylla Brodzinsky, Max Schoening
from Colombians Displaced by Violence
Surviving Justice: America's Wrongfully .... Eds. Dave Eggers, Lola Vollen
Convicted and Exonerated
Palestine Speaks: Narratives of Life under Occupation ..... Eds. Mateo Hoke and Cate Malek
Nowhere to Be Home: Narratives from .... Eds. Maggie Lemere, Zoë West
Survivors of Burma's Military Regime
Refugee Hotel .... Juliet Linderman, Gabriele Stabile
Patriot Acts: Narratives of Post-9/11 Injustice .... Ed. Alia Malek
Underground America: Narratives of Undocumented Lives .... Ed. Peter Orner
Hope Deferred: Narratives of Zimbabwean Lives .... Eds. Peter Orner, Annie Holmes
High Rise Stories: Voices from Chicago Public Housing .... Ed. Audrey Petty
Inside This Place, Not of It: .... Eds. Ayelet Waldman, Robin Levi
Narratives from Women's Prisons
Out of Exile: Narratives from the .... Ed. Craig Walzer
Abducted and Displaced People of Sudan
Voices from the Storm .... Eds. Chris Ying, Lola Vollen

HUMOR

The Secret Language of Sleep .... Amelia Bauer, Evany Thomas
Baby Do My Banking .... Lisa Brown
Baby Fix My Car .... Lisa Brown
Baby Get Me Some Lovin' .... Lisa Brown
Baby Make Me Breakfast .... Lisa Brown
Baby Plan My Wedding .... Lisa Brown
Comedy by the Numbers .... Eric Hoffman, Gary Rudoren
The Emily Dickinson Reader .... Paul Legault
All Known Metal Bands .... Dan Nelson
How to Dress for Every Occasion .... The Pope
The Latke Who Couldn't Stop Screaming .... Lemony Snicket, Lisa Brown
The Future Dictionary of America .... Various
I Found This Funny .... Various; Ed. Judd Apatow
I Live Real Close to Where You Used to Live .... Various; Ed. Lauren Hall
Thanks and Have Fun Running the Country .... Various; Ed. Jory John
The Best of McSweeney's Internet Tendency .... Various; Ed. Chris Monks, John Warner

POETRY

City of Rivers .... Zubair Ahmed
Remains .... Jesús Castillo
The Boss .... Victoria Chang
x .... Dan Chelotti
Tombo .... W. S. Di Piero
Flowers of Anti-Martyrdom .... Dorian Geisler
Of Lamb .... Matthea Harvey; Ill. Amy Jean Porter
The Abridged History of Rainfall .... Jay Hopler
Love, an Index .... Rebecca Lindenberg
Fragile Acts .... Allan Peterson
In the Shape of a Human Body .... Various; Eds. Ilya Kaminsky,
I Am Visiting the Earth   Dominic Luxford, Jesse Nathan
The McSweeney's Book of Poets Picking Poets .... Various; Ed. Dominic Luxford

COLLINS LIBRARY

Curious Men .... Frank Buckland
Lunatic at Large .... J. Storer Clouston
The Rector and the Rogue .... W. A. Swanberg

ALL THIS AND MORE AT
STORE.MCSWEENEYS.NET

Imagine it: a four-issue subscription to *McSweeney's Quarterly*.

Four issues, for $95.
store.mcsweeneys.net

Founded in 1998, McSweeney's is an independent publisher based in San Francisco. McSweeney's exists to champion ambitious and inspired new writing, and to challenge conventional expectations about where it's found, how it looks, and who participates. We're here to discover things we love, help them find their most resplendent form, and place them into the hands of curious, engaged readers.

THERE ARE SEVERAL WAYS TO SUPPORT McSWEENEY'S:

Support Us on Patreon
visit www.patreon.com/mcsweeneysinternettendency

Subscribe & Shop
visit store.mcsweeneys.net

Volunteer & Intern
email eric@mcsweeneys.net

Sponsor Books & Quarterlies
email amanda@mcsweeneys.net

To learn more, please visit *www.mcsweeneys.net/donate*
or contact Executive Director Amanda Uhle at
amanda@mcsweeneys.net or 415.642.5609.

McSweeney's Literary Arts Fund is a non-profit organization.
Contributions to McSweeney's are tax deductible to
the extent permitted by law.